1987

... a year of EXCESS ...

PAUL MITCHELL

Book Publishing.com

Design, typesetting and publishing by UK Book Publishing

www.ukbookpublishing.com

ISBN: 978-1-916572-83-6

1987

... a year of EXCESS ...

INTRODUCTION

A lthough chronologically this book is only three years away from George Orwell's classic, there is little similarity between his seminal, prophetic work and my romp through Capital Markets in the eighties. If I could describe this book, I would call it a memory box. People bury these things from time to time with a content that is supposed to conjure up a picture of what life was like at that moment in time. This book has been buried in me effectively and I am now opening it.

The City at that time was a cauldron of racism, misogyny, homophobia, bullying and unadulterated greed. I don't believe in sanitising events and whilst the sentiments expressed by some of the characters are reprehensible, I believe they accurately represent attitudes held by a good number of participants in the market.

In 1987, was I,

Racist? Never

Misogynistic? No, but a little sexist.

Homophobic? Those days, probably yes.

A bully? No

Greedy? A relative concept I think and best judged by someone else. A need to make money was integral to my job. I'm not the best person to ask!

The characters contained within are all imaginary, save a minor one (who was too lovable to change) and are constructed to suit the events I describe. Characters may have facets of people I worked with but are certainly not meant to represent any real-life individuals. Halfway through writing this book I attended a Veteran's football lunch and got talking to some old rivals about the book I was writing. I invented a broker called "Grub" because I had heard a colleague of mine call down his box to one called "Slug" and thought "Grub "would be an even better name than "Slug" for my imaginary broker. On revealing this to the table, some of whom had been in the money markets, they said "Yes we remember Grub". They then proceed to tell me that they had a broker going by this nickname in their markets in the 80's!

Rightly or wrongly, I liked the name so much I was loath to change it. So, let me assure him, and any readers of this book, I have never met this man, I first heard of him in about 2019, and NOTHING attributed to my character in this book is a reflection of, or a reference to, the real-life person or to Slug for that matter. Similarly Regal Bank is not meant to represent any particular institution... "Regal" is merely an anagram of large.

The events I write about didn't happen as described here. Things similar to these events have been recounted to me, or I have witnessed myself, but I have tampered with them all to fit into a story line. I actually went to a Frank Sinatra concert at the Albert Hall, but it was in 1989. I've exaggerated the move in treasuries in October to make the problem with the SNCF look worse. I'm not even sure SNCF ever issued any callable 10-year bonds. There are a multitude of other factual errors if you take this book as an accurate record of actual events.

It is NOT! It's fiction.

I suppose a good question is "what did I want to achieve by writing this?"

I'm not entirely sure to be honest but the stories seemed to always be bursting to get out of me and the only way I could exorcise the demons was to get it all down on paper. After how I have described the City back then it seems terrible to say I mostly enjoyed it. I guess thirty years of it would have been tough if I didn't derive some enjoyment along the way. Critics could say it was alright for me because I was white, male and heterosexual, all of which is true and equally unchangeable. I like to think in my behaviour towards the people I encountered in the market, I treated them as I wanted to be treated.

What do I want the reader to gain from this? If it makes any sense, I'd put it like this.

"It's not a real roast dinner, but if you digest it, you'll hopefully know exactly how one tastes!"

CHAPTER 1

It had been some years since John Field had really enjoyed a Christmas break, and this one had seemed to stretch on for an interminable length of time due to New Year's Day being on a Thursday. Although markets were open on the Friday, his bank told him he could take the day off for free to spend with his family so John, unwilling to admit that it was the last place he wanted to be, quietly acquiesced. That was all history now anyway, it was Monday and John was eagerly anticipating his return to the office, a place where his stature was more recognised, and he was given the type of respect he deserved. A place where he would not be constantly badgered about "settling down" and where people would know that the expensive wine he had bought for the family was not actually pronounced "Chabliss".

He checked himself in the full-length mirror before leaving his flat, chuckling inwardly to himself that he might ever wear either of the M & S shirts his parents had given him as presents. John's choice of suit was a strident Prince of Wales check coupled with a blue shirt with a white collar. The January weather meant he would also scoop up his trench coat on the way out and slip into his regulation footwear, a pair of Charles Church brogues. John was very proud of his shoes and had further improved them (in his mind), by having large steel heel tips fitted on both pairs he owned. When John was approaching on the marble floored atria of city buildings there was no element of surprise. It sounded something like a squadron of Waffen SS on the march. He could vividly remember when he first went into a shoe shop and saw them. He was with an old school friend who had audibly swallowed when he heard the price of them and blurted out "fuck me, Churches, I'd want a pair of Cathedrals for that money!". The opportunity to impress his old friend had been too much to pass up and John waved his hand towards his body in the universal buying gesture common to the market and said to the kneeling shop assistant "mine, I'll have two pairs."

As he walked down the three stone steps out of his converted Victorian townhouse to the street level, he mulled whether to walk to the tube station or jump in a cab. The immediate throbbing of a diesel engine and a bright orange light shining through the early morning gloom soon made his mind up and he whistled through his teeth and shouted "Copthall Avenue please mate" through the half open window. His destination was the offices of his employers, Regal Bank.

He had been head-hunted there after just eighteen months on the dealing desk at Ambrose Bank where he had spent all his working life, progressing from back-office duties to a place on the front desk due to his undeniable talent. That was John's take on it anyway...the occurrence of a team move to another company by 75% of the Regal Bank front office some weeks earlier may, in reality, have had more to do with it.

The hiring of the Regal Bank team in 1985 was by no means a solitary event. The deregulation of the City, or "Big Bang" as it became known, brought about huge changes in the City. U.S. banks in particular were some of the most aggressive entrants to stake a claim on long established British brands and the subsequent demand for experienced trading personnel meant a much appreciated, (by the front office workers anyway) spiral upwards in hiring and remuneration. Traders were changing jobs with alarming regularity and the practice of immediately telling anyone who wanted to hire you that you were on at least 25% more than you actually earned became an almost pavlovian response. This had caused some embarrassment for John on his first day at Regal Bank when he was going through formalities with the head of Personnel, Humphrey Black-Hawkins. It was patently clear to John when he interviewed for the job that he was persona non grata with Humphrey. The head of trading had told John "We have to wheel you past Black-Hawkins for form's sake but don't take any notice of the wanker ...he's got no say in it".

Black-Hawkins had adopted a feigned interest in John's moderate academic achievements at his North London Grammar School and had also shown great surprise at the fact that Latin had been taught there...a preserve surely, he thought, of only the more privileged educational establishments. Thatcher and the yanks were ruining the city and here was another example of it in his mind. He'd even heard in the executive dining room that brokers were hiring people who had left school at 16. What was his world coming to?

As his head of trading had said, Black-Hawkins had no say in it, and John was duly hired on a salary of £120,000 p.a. being £20,000 above what he had told Regal Bank he was earning at Ambrose. There was some embarrassment on his induction day with Black-Hawkins due to the fact that his P60 end of employment tax declaration showed his actual salary had been £47,000. Embarrassment is perhaps too strong a word for someone of John's psychological make up, and when questioned about it by Black-Hawkins his response was at first to waffle on about bonuses being taken into account and then, in a practically blatant admission of his subterfuge he finished with "well you wouldn't want someone trading bonds for you who can't negotiate would you?"

The taxi pulled up outside the Regal Bank building and John aimed a £10 note through the partition and said "keep the change mate" as he narrowly avoided a puddle getting out of the cab. The large 10 storey stone-clad building was in a neo-classical style with all the windows coated in a non-reflective covering. Regal Bank had the top four floors and as John walked in through the revolving doors he remembered that steel tipped, leather soled shoes could be somewhat slippery on marble floors when it had been raining so he carefully crabbed over to the lifts past the dozing security guard who manned the reception desk up until 8.30 a.m. Regal Bank were obviously economizing on heating as he noticed a thee bar electric fire glowing on the floor of the reception desk underneath the guard's outstretched legs. John waved his pass at the security panel on the lift, got in and pressed "10".

The trading floor was a vast open-plan space with the trading desks set in a big horse-shoe arc so that staff were sitting looking at one another either side of the horseshoe with a high-level valley in between them. The high-level valley was actually a conveyor belt for tickets. On writing a ticket the trader would throw the ticket into the valley, where the conveyor would take it all the way round to a desk where the input clerk would time stamp the ticket and enter it into the system. Pink for a sale and Blue for a buy. Chloe and Michelle were the trusty input girls and John wondered what time they had to get up in Romford to turn up for the start of trading looking as neatly coiffured as they always did.

The majority of the chairs in the trading room were of a tired looking green, heavy weave material that attempted to match the grey/green weave in the carpet tiles. John made his way to the black leather chair in the middle of the horseshoe that he had specifically requested from the facilities guy and hooked his jacket over the inbuilt hanger fixed into the back of the chair. Although he had insisted upon the executive model chair, he would in hindsight have preferred one of the material ones because the thing was so slippery, he had trouble maintaining an upright posture, but there was no way he was going to admit it. Consequently, he spent significant parts of the day standing up which had its advantages when it came to poking your nose into the comings and goings on the trading floor...you couldn't see over the conveyor belt when seated.

"Happy New Year John!" trilled a cheerful voice from the other side of the room. Nicola was one of the few people who got in as early as John, and she entered from the opposite side of the trading floor because she regularly liked to walk up the 20 flights of stairs. "Yep, same to you Nic, another day another dollar eh? You walked off all the Christmas pud up them stairs?"

"Oooh don't, I feel the size of a house" she replied as she slipped her coat off and onto a hook on the wall behind her and took her seat in the sales section of the trading arc. John generally had a dismissive attitude towards any "spoons" he came across in the industry. In his classification of spoons, he included anyone who pronounced their "th's", anyone with a house with more than four bedrooms, and a special category of people who pronounced "issue" like it was spelled rather than "ishoo". Nicola qualified because not long after he met her, she told him she was moving house.

"How many bedrooms has your new house got then?" John grilled her bluntly.

Without any hint of pretentiousness, she replied "Do you know I haven't actually counted!"

John didn't need to hear her pronunciation of Issue after this confession, and she was quickly promoted to aristocracy in his view. Despite this he developed a grudging admiration for her irrepressible optimism and good humour and found her a great colleague to work with and had even given up insulting her. Nicola Avery was a spoon, Humphrey Black-Hawkins was a spoon and Rupert De Villiers was definitely a spoon, but the latter was John's head of trading and the polar opposite of the ex-Navy head of personnel. It was Rupert who had hired John to Regal Bank and if anything, he seemed to have a preference for hiring traders from non-traditional backgrounds. As the floor started to fill up, they started dribbling in.

Next through the door was Ron Harris, affectionately known as "Chopper" after the notorious Chelsea full-back of the same name. Chopper was another of Rupert's "rough diamond "hires. A Southend resident with a penchant for cockney rhyming slang, although most of his slang had been invented by Chopper himself to make it sound like he'd spent his life in Brick Lane. "A bit plate of skate this morning son. Wanted to get in George Birley" was a fine example. The fact that the majority of the people working in the city, would not have known the difference, allied with the fact that Chopper was in the habit of slurring his words together, meant that most people found him only semi-intelligible before lunch. Chopper was also a hopeless drunk, so post-lunch you were lucky if you got every fifth word. His long-suffering wife seemed to have an inbuilt sensor for when he had been out to one of his long lunches and would call in to the office about 5 minutes after he had returned...usually around the 4.15 p.m. mark.

"Hello Ron, you been to lunch?"

"Mmm"

"You pissed again?"

"nnnn"

"You think by not saying any actual words I can't tell you're pissed?"

"ermm"

The conversation was normally terminated at this point unless Ron wanted to prove his restraint by protesting "no stickies though", which meant his lunch had not progressed to the bottle of Port stage.

Chopper was in Rupert's fantasy three. Rupert had an agreement to pay money to a charity if Chopper and his two mates, who were on the broking side of the business, all made it in before 7.30 on a Friday morning. As Thursday nights were big nights in the City, Rupert's bank account had only been troubled twice in the previous year.

"Alright Fieldy son?" was Chopper's greeting. He called everyone son, so John had given up reminding him he was slightly older than him.

"Where's Gazza?"

"I'm not his fucking mother" replied John. "He's supposed to be back today".

As if on cue Gary Davis arrived from the lift entrance in a rather fetching camel overcoat that John swore he had last seen on the character "Flash Harry", the spiv from the St Trinian's movies.

"Oi oi!" piped up John. He was already tiring from the strain of keeping his body upright on the glossy leather seat and was on his feet when Gary entered." Who's got a new Christmas coat then? Did you get a soap on a rope too from mummy?"

The dark-eyed look from Gary told John he had gone far enough for the moment with someone who had a notorious temper and had actually punched a client on a night out.

Gary had been at Regal Bank when John started but only preceded him by a week or so. They first met when John caught sight of him reading Country Life, the celebrated magazine of the hunting/shooting /fishing caste. As he walked past the seated trader, he noticed he was looking at a property advertisement for a large house near Chelmsford. The aerial view of the place was the main picture and it looked stunning. A tennis court and a walled garden with a large swimming pool were all on view and John ventured "you thinking of buying the place?"

Gary looked up and paused for a moment before replying "nah, I used to deliver the milk there!"

This was a bit of a non sequitur and John wandered back to his desk wondering how shocked Humphrey Black-Hawkins must have been when Rupert wheeled an ex-milkman through his doors.

The desk intercom beeped into life and Nicola's voice was piped all around the room announcing, "morning meeting", a signal for all the floor to gather in the inside of the horseshoe and exchange views on the day ahead.

The morning meeting was an innovation brought in by the American bosses of Regal Bank. John hated it, as he did most things American. If you've got anything smart to say why wait until 7.45 a.m. the next morning? In his mind it had become merely a vehicle for their economist to pontificate on various theories and use words that Chopper, Gazza and himself didn't understand and wouldn't have traded on even if they did. Economists occupied a special area of hatred in John's mind. Anyone who regularly used words like "Panglossian" and prefaced everything they said about the day before with "as expected" was, to put it in Chopper's parlance, "about as much use as a chocolate fireguard".

You had to play the game though, and the salespeople seemed to like it if you could give them a strong opinion of where you thought the market was going to go for the day. John's cynical side told him what they really wanted was the ability to chisel away at his prices, if he said he thought the market was going down then they would complain if he wasn't the best offer .He'd got around it by asking one of his brokers to send him regular economic snippets that he could read out at the meetings to appear as if he was plugged in to all things dollar denominated. Today it was the U.S. Federal budget being presented to Congress. Having said his piece, he switched himself to neutral as Vince McDonnell, the desk economist, launched into his usual spiel. He'd obviously been doing a bit of revision over the holiday period as this morning's obscure word was "lucubration". John had not the slightest interest in what this word meant and was pretty sure he had no need to insert a word into his vocabulary that would just send anyone listening scrambling for dictionaries. "New Year, same old shit" he thought to himself. The concerted movement of people up from where they had been perching for the meeting prompted John out of his reverie and he marched purposefully back to his desk. There were things to do. He was going to have a good start to the year; this wasn't unbridled optimism on his part but a knowledge that towards the end of last year, when his bonus had more or less been decided, he had started to mark down some of his holdings of bonds. Although you were supposed to mark your bonds to market at the end of the year, and the back office were supposed to check them, in reality it was tough for them to find out where they should have been and by the time they actually realised he had mis-marked them he would have marked them back to the correct price. The intervening period would be covered by him blustering "the bonds are where I say they are...that's why I'm called a market-maker you mugboat". Traders were humoured by the banks in this practice, particularly if they were making money and back-office checks were seen as a minor, but unavoidable nuisance. Rupert, his boss, was nobody's fool and he knew what was going on, but as long as the mismark was below market value you could always say you were being "conservative". Anyway, it did Rupert no harm if his traders all shot out of the blocks at the start of the year and John firmly believed you could trade better if there was a "bit of money in the bin early doors".

So, as he settled down to the first trading day of the year John's main concern was how much money he was going to make today and on which issues. 1987 was going to be good!

CHAPTER 2

J anuary 5th was Steve Perkins' first day back in the office too. Unlike John Field he loved the Christmas break and unlike most people, saw it as a chance to eat a little less than his normal working life demanded. Many people in Steve's family would scarcely have believed he was practicing restraint in his yuletide feasting, but his consumption at work was on a truly industrial scale. It was perhaps for this reason, or maybe the concertina folds of his stomach that resembled something found on a lettuce leaf that he had earned the nickname "Grub". At the age of 32 he had come to accept that he wasn't going to get slimmer anytime soon, but he liked to think he was sacrificing his body for his work. He compared it to being a jockey. They had to go without food to earn their money, he had to eat a hell a lot of it with customers to earn his money. He had worked at Plummer's brokerage for 10 years now and would perhaps have moved on if he hadn't had been such good friends with the boss. They had both grown up together in Bethnal Green and he felt even if he was considering a better offer, he would have to tell Kev about it first. Plummer's were brokers; they put together buyers and sellers and took a small commission on the way through. As such they were blissfully indifferent to whether the market was going up or down, but their profits were directly related to how much turnover there was. As one could imagine any new product, currency or innovation in the market was gleefully looked upon as just another chance to take brokerage or "bro". With a business plan like this it's not hard to see that traders who did a lot of business would be worth a lot to Plummer's, and to encourage them not to do their business elsewhere, the proportion of profits spent on entertainment was considerable. Steve Perkins lolled back in his chair and surveyed his stomach, pulling on the buttons of his starched white shirt. John Field was his best account and at least one of Grub's bellies could be solely blamed on him.

Plummer's premises were somewhat less grand than Regal Bank's. Located in White's Row, technically a City location, it was Whitechapel to most people. In fact, one of Jack the Ripper's victims was thought to have been killed there and Grub found it ironic that, 100 years later, if he came in very early in the morning (or very late from the night before) he would normally pass one or two working ladies with pallid complexions and haunted eyes asking him "looking for business love?" He would always politely decline but Grub was not philosophically opposed to a bit of "retail trade" as he liked to call it and had actually made a habit of preaching to younger brokers about the moral dilemma of whether to pay for sex or not. Grub's equivalent of the old adage "may as well be hung for a sheep as a lamb" was "if you're gonna pay for it, you may as well have two!". Shoreditch streetwalkers were not his bag, but he was easily tempted by more upmarket offerings.

The modus operandi in Plummer's was a lot different to Regal Bank. If there was a morning meeting it was to decide who went for the bacon rolls the other side of Commercial Street. If anyone got in after 7.30 a.m., they had to go, but as all the brokers had turned up bright eyed and bushy tailed after enforced time at home, the spoof game had to start. Spoof was a regular way of deciding things like this, and the penalty was normally to pay for something. Each player was allowed between three and zero coins in his hand and then all players extended their closed fist out into the middle of the circle they were standing in and took guesses at the total number. Anyone who guessed the right number was out and so inevitably it would come down to two players. Early exits were generally just luck, but when it came down to the final, it was best of three, and if Veg was in the final you knew you were safe. Veg's real name was Terry Wilson. If ignorance was bliss Terry was very happy. Grub knew why he was a good broker, he very rarely offered opinions on things, was as level-headed and cheerful as a person could possibly be and he could drink like a fish. Early in his career he had struck up a friendship with a very unlikely entrant to the broking game, Gerald Donat. Gerald was anything but your archetypal broker. He went to RADA when he left school and still harboured dreams of becoming a stage actor. His entrance into broking had come as a necessity after his father got into trouble with a stock market investment and he felt the need to do something more financially rewarding. His best friend at school had gone straight into the City and had started becoming fantastically successful. One night he told Gerald that if he went to work for the broker, he would pass all his business through him. When he told his parents about the chance, he could see the conflict in his mother's eyes. She knew what was in Gerald's heart but was also worried about the family house. Gerald accepted his friend's offer and now eight years later he had got used to the money. His father's fortunes had recovered, and the family house was no longer at risk. He had a rolling horizon for when he would throw it all in and go back to acting, but as he admitted to himself, it was always two years away. In the testosterone charged atmosphere of the brokerage house his cultured accent, theatrical ways, and his failure to take a copy of the Sun to the toilet with him soon had him marked down as "the homo in the corner". Gerald wasn't gay, but the energy he would have had to expend denying it, was just not worth the effort and he didn't see the need to parade his girlfriend around the City to prove it. On Gerald's first day at Plummer's, he was seated next to Terry Wilson. The choice was a purposeful one made by their boss Kevin Connolly as he thought Terry was the least likely to have any problems with sitting next to someone so alien to the majority of the people in the room. So, Gerald had a wall on one side and someone only slightly more understanding on the other side. Against all odds, their friendship seemed to work out. Gerald's schoolfriend was as good as his word and "the homo in the corner" was soon outproducing most of the room. Someone coined the term for the twosome "fruit and veg" and from then on that was how they were known. It looked like another genius move by Kevin to pair them up and in a way, it was a decision he was rightly proud of. He wasn't the boss just because he had some of the best contacts; he knew that successful broking needed a buyer AND a seller and if you only had half the trade, you did nothing. A variety of personalities in his brokerage ensured that he could get into some of the more eccentric characters in the market, and their volumes were just as good as anyone else's.

The spoof game had reached its climax. In what was an auspicious start to the New Year, Veg had managed to avoid the final which the guys called Mano a Mano. Veg assumed this was Spanish for man to man and cheerfully watched as Grub completely foxed a younger opponent 2-0 and proceeded to trot out the details of the full English breakfast he wanted. With the formalities out of the way the brokers resumed their seats and started putting calls into their clients.

There was no complicated strategy in approaching the first contact of the day with your client. "Hello mate, have a nice Christmas?" was a welcome alternative to the normal Monday "Hello mate, have a nice weekend?". The more established brokers would wait until their clients were ready to furnish them with a couple of starting prices whereas the younger, more paranoid guys would be on the lines from 8.01 a.m. Grub meticulously chased the last piece of sausage around the polystyrene container his breakfast had come in making sure he scraped up the remnants of the third brown sauce sachet with it. A speaker in front of him crackled into life and John Field's unmistakeable North London accent came through the box "Oi! you finished your breakfast yet? I want some prices". With a resigned shrug, Grub flipped himself forward from the semi-prone position he had just adopted to aid the digestion of his breakfast, threw the old breakfast box into a nearby bin and pressed the red light on the speaker in front of him. "Morning Fieldy, was just on a call getting some for you...back in a second." He immediately resumed his laid-back stance and shouted in the general direction of the remaining brokers "come on you fuckers, I need some prices!" before flipping open his copy of the Sun on the sport section. If the worst came to the worst, he would do what he normally did; make some up. Technically brokers were not supposed to run positions as they generally would not have the ability to pay for them, but Grub had been in the market some time now and knew that traders rarely traded on the first price they saw and on the odd occasion that he did get hit or lifted he could usually get a friendly trader to take him out of the position for the price of a good lunch. Also, the company wouldn't have to find any cash to fund an intraday position, so as long as they were out of it before the end of day, there was no harm done. This policy had provided a few hairy moments for Grub and Kevin in the past, but overall, it was certainly justifiable. Grub knew his best clients' major positions well, so his favourite ploy was to give what he knew was a poor bid in something the trader was long of. "EIB 9.5 are 99 bid Fieldy" was usually followed by something like "that's a shit bid Grub, I'm 99.25 bid myself". As he knew where Fieldy wanted to sell them, he now had a two way price working. "I'm 99 and a quarter three quarters EIB 9 and a half's" he would shout in stentorian tones to the room. With a puff of the cheeks, indicating what great efforts Grub had made to establish the price, and a searching look around the rest of the brokers, he would then flip back in his seat silently broadcasting, "I've done my bit, now you lot have to pull your fingers out".

Grub wouldn't be making any prices up today; he hadn't seen any prices since December 19th so didn't have a clue where they should be or how the traders worked them out. He'd never really admitted to it but after 10 years in the market he still had a very limited understanding of what he was broking. It could have been potatoes for all he cared. All that mattered was that the there was a buyer and a seller and in putting them together there was profit.

His knowledge was of people's psychology, their fear and greed, and that was universal, be it potatoes or bonds.

Anyway, after a period of relatively healthy eating Grub felt the need to start looking ahead to lunchtime. He guessed Fieldy would be feeling the same. Chopper had told him once that it was "unprofessional to talk about lunch before 9.30". This tickled Grub as Chopper presumably considered it very professional to sink a bottle of Port at lunchtime and then return to the office for some inspired trading. However, he would wait until after the watershed to suggest the Doctor Butler's Head to Fieldy where the Steak and Kidney pie was served by the shovel load and the Guinness flowed.

So, much like any other year, this was how 1987 started in Plummer's.

CHAPTER 3

Not for the first time, Delroy's nose wrinkled at the acrid smell of urine in the lift. He pressed the "G" button and waited for the door to shut. When five seconds had elapsed without movement, he decided on his second option, a small jump in the air which shook the lift and seemed to encourage the door to come to life again. With a noise worthy of a machine twice its size the door creaked shut and its journey to the ground floor began. As he left the lift, he plotted a course hugging tight to the wall of the block of flats so as to avoid the worst of the January rain pounding down that morning. He might normally have sprinted to the garage but an over eager full-back in Saturday's game had given him a dead leg and his thigh felt like there was a huge knot in it. His garage was located in a row of ten, underneath the children's recreation park. When he finally reached his garage, he swiftly unlocked it and flipped the up and over door into position and took cover. He whipped out a large handkerchief from his back pocket and mopped his face dry. A fleeting memory crossed his mind of his early dancing days when a mopping down was an absolute necessity after dancing to "The Hustle", and a large handkerchief in the back pocket was as much of a uniform as the high waist band trousers and an afro fork stuck in the back of his hair. He smiled to himself wondering how much "hustling" he'd be doing with his thigh the way it was and thanked his lucky stars he had a sedentary job.

As usual, Delroy's cab was sparkling. After a couple of tries the engine spluttered into life and the familiar clatter of a diesel engine occupied the space. As he edged the cab forward so that he could close the garage door he mused, as he had done many times before, how much a remote-control opener would cost. By the time he'd closed the door and got back in the cab the thought had passed and would remain forgotten until the next inclement morning.

He knew he was lucky to have a garage. The council flat he lived in was on the third floor, which was the top floor, of a large development built in the late 60's. He could remember moving in like it was yesterday. The house his family had lived in until he was eight was knocked down in what they called "slum clearance" and had been a cold, inhospitable place, with the only heating being the open fires in the main rooms. The outside toilet in the backyard was daunting in winter and the condensation on the inside of the windows at night could have irrigated a whole field of rice. The new flats had a communal heating system that was all included in the rent, so from 1968 onwards Delroy's family lived in sub-tropical temperatures through the whole year. The existence of a garage with the property came as a surprise to them and as they didn't have a car, the temptation to say, "is the rent cheaper if we don't take the garage?" was strong. In the end Delroy's dad decided he could make a bit of a man-cave of it and tried his hand at manufacturing some home-brew. The home-brew tasted vile but there were always a few bottles of Wray and Nephew stacked at the back as a standby. The addition of a couple of armchairs and a coffee table made it an ideal spot for dominoes with his mates on occasional Sundays. His dad had died when he was 14 and when Delroy had first got a moped, then later qualified as a Black Cab driver, he had cleared the brewing equipment and furniture and finally used the garage for its designated purpose.

He no longer paid rent for the garage or his flat. Under the "Right to Buy "legislation his mother was able to buy their flat for a fraction of its market value and Delroy had happily supplied the cash to his mum as she was returning to Saint Lucia where her family were from, and his two younger sisters had relocated with her. He had no doubt at some time he would be able to make a lot of money by selling the place but for the moment he was exactly where he wanted to be geographically, and life was good.

He sat stationary in the cab for a good five minutes waiting for the clatter to die down to a more bearable throb. His normal route would take him to Liverpool Street, where a steady flow of City workers getting off

mainline trains would provide a reliable supply of fares...
especially in the rain.

He wasn't entirely sure how he'd ended up in this
profession. His early academic career was promising, and
he was playing youth team football with a professional club
up until the age of 14 but the events surrounding his father's
death were cataclysmic. His father was a lot older than his
mother and when he died suddenly in a road accident his
death triggered a series of events that dramatically changed
Delroy's outlook on life and his perception of who he was.
Before the funeral his mum had confessed to him that
Reginald was not his true biological father, and that his
real father was a Jamaican who his mum had had a short-
term liaison with. Reginald had always been an admirer of
Marta's and having been brought up a strict catholic, she
persuaded him to marry her as soon as she realised she was
carrying Delroy and travelled to England. Reginald always
seemed harder on Delroy than his two sisters. Marta was
never sure whether this was because he suspected the baby
wasn't his or just a paternal preference for girls, but if he did
suspect anything there was never a mention of it.

The revelation threw up a myriad of questions in
Delroy's mind. School work was the first thing to suffer,
and in a seemingly unrelated event he was dropped from
the youth team. He knew he was better than most of the
players on the squad but had been late out of the changing
rooms after one session and heard the two coaches
discussing things.

"Yea, he's got good skills, but I'm worried about that black attitude thing" was the head coach's contribution.

The reply to this was somewhat muffled but Delroy clearly heard "chip on his shoulder".

"Think I prefer someone with a bit less skill but a lot more graft" continued the first voice.

Delroy kissed his teeth, a part of him hoping they might hear him and walked out of the dressing room almost sure his days there were over and thinking "50 million population, a wide ethnic mix, and football's our national sport. Until we get some continental coaches over here, getting their hands on young kids and teaching them properly, England won't win a thing. The population of Holland is about 12 million for Christ's sake".

In the subsequent months he spent more of his time around the flats where a little gang of first generation West Indian kids hung about and less and less of his time doing homework. This transition did not go unnoticed by his teachers and mother, but Delroy felt with the betrayal she had revealed to him, she was in no position to lecture. He was angry as hell but didn't really have a focal point for that anger. His new mates had a hierarchy, and he had to establish himself in that hierarchy. He was strong, athletically built and with the anger burning within him it only took a few scraps to establish himself as someone not to be messed with. He'd even fought and subdued a white gang member from Hoxton, although he didn't know who he was at the time. The two had become firm friends since and Delroy was still in contact with him.

The events following Reginald's death also led him to do some deep thinking. Delroy liked to allow himself periods of time to just mull things over in his head. He would challenge himself to defend ideas that would seem indefensible, question the accepted norm, effectively say "why not" to anything and then try to find supporting rationale for a seemingly unconventional viewpoint. He had started thinking more about the black-white thing. The catholic school his mother insisted on sending him to had a high proportion of Irish descended kids there and Reginald had joked when he went there "you're with your kind. When I first came here, they had signs on the lodging houses "No Blacks, No Irish". He had started in school thinking the path to success would be through academic success and a good job. He'd even had piano lessons for two years. Now he started thinking "am I just playing a game by the white man's rules?". He felt he could get all the qualifications in the world but attitudes like he'd heard from the two football coaches would be insurmountable obstacles to entering their world. Even if you did manage to enter it, were you selling out? As he read somewhere once: "even if you're winning the rat race, you're still a rat".

These thoughts had coalesced in his mind for some years, and he wouldn't have been Delroy Joseph if he didn't, at some time, test whether that theory stood up to his analysis. Five years of running with the rude boys round the flats had brought him involvement in criminal activities and he started considering whether he was just now conforming to a black stereotype. Single mother, no father to discipline an unruly son, he was turning into one of the "yout" his mother used to single out as examples of bad upbringing, it would all culminate in doing some prison time somewhere, a path that once embarked upon was very difficult to withdraw from.

By the age of 19, he concluded he should quietly back out of gang life and a chance comment from the manager of his under 14's East London District side had always stuck with him. "Any cab driver who says he is not well off is either lazy or lying".

So, Delroy got back into his football, started playing semi-professionally in the Isthmian league, bought a moped, and started "the knowledge". The knowledge is the name for the qualification process for all London black cab drivers. Prospective drivers have to prove their knowledge of the routes in the "Blue Book" (which was actually Pink), to an examiner and depending on their success they were called back after a varying number of days from 56's to 21's. Anyone on 21's was getting close to getting his badge. The examiners' reputation was fearsome. The combined effect of having to remember a lot of information whilst not reacting to deliberate provocation from them was enough to make a quivering wreck of the biggest of men. The assessments were made at the London Carriage Office in Penton Street, Islington and Delroy thought he would come to blows at his very first one. After waiting nervously in an ante room, he was summoned by a bull-chested examiner called Mr Graves. He followed the examiner down a long, polished parquet flooring corridor into his office where there was a small chair facing a desk bearing the name Mr Graves printed on Dymo letter tape with a rather grander chair behind it.

He sat on the small chair but before his full weight had settled into it, Mr Graves bellowed "did I tell you to sit down?". Delroy bounced up again swiftly and bit his lip. "OK, sit down now".

The route tests were all passed flawlessly, and Delroy didn't get to see Mr Graves again until what he hoped was going to be his final assessment. If anything, Mr Graves seemed even surlier on this exam, throwing in some race related slurs as well as his normal provocative banter. At the end of it all Mr Graves suddenly smiled, reached his hand out to him and shook it warmly. "Congratulations Mr Joseph you've got your badge!" Delroy had been concentrating so much on keeping a poker face that he perhaps didn't exhibit as much joy as he was feeling but managed a "thanks Mr Graves" in response. "Sorry about all the insults" the examiner continued, "but you could get it when you're out and about from ignorant members of the public and we try hard to make sure you're not the type of person to lose your rag".

The cab seemed to have reached operating temperature, Delroy flipped open the case of cassettes he had in the empty section next to his driving seat. He was quite fussy about his music and had installed a top of the range radio/cassette player in his cab. With the weather looking so grim he needed something to make him feel warm and cosy. After some indecision he opted for the tape entitled "Lover's Rock" and slid it into the Alpine. You couldn't listen to Lover's Rock or Reggae without feeling the bass line. At the Four Aces in Dalston, a dance hall where he went sometimes, the massive speakers made his chest vibrate. The large woofers he'd had installed in the cab kicked into action and the familiar intro to Janet Kay's "Silly Games" started. Delroy put the cab into "drive", eased the pedal down and edged onto the road whilst attempting a falsetto #I've been wanting you, for so long, it's a shame#.

Even a full-blooded attack from Mr Graves would have trouble upsetting his equilibrium today.

CHAPTER 4

You weren't sure it was Friday morning in the City unless you had at least a bit of a hangover. Rupert sipped on the strong coffee he'd picked up from the hole in the wall across the street on the way in and felt the slight haze from last night's cocktails gradually dissipate. He opened the P and L reports for the first few days of the year that had been printed off in an overnight run and left on his desk. Things were looking OK, but he had been doing this long enough to not get too excited about a couple of good days. He would allow himself a bit of self-congratulation if things were this good come December the 15th perhaps but for the moment, he consoled himself with "better up than down on the first week". It was no surprise to him that John's book was showing up a considerable amount, but closer scrutiny would show this was all unrealized profit, and in fact the realized column of his P and L showed he'd lost a little money trading but the large mark up of his long positions meant he was well up on the week. As many wizened traders had commented in the past "It's not a maths exam", meaning you got no marks for using the right method.... the right answer was all people cared about at the end of the day. Running through a mental "in-tray" his next pending task was to find out if he was going be contributing to charity this week. He could see Chopper was in already and he'd heard Grub shouting through the box, if Frank Robinson was in too, the Great Ormond Street charity would be receiving a £50 contribution.

"Fieldy, you heard from Robbo yet this morning?" he enquired.

"I doubt if you'll hear much from him this morning guv, he was last spotted with some treacle in the Aquarius about midnight."

The Aquarius Club was a notorious hangout in the West-end. Scantily clad ladies would encourage punters to buy sparkling Perry with a fancy label for the price of a magnum of Dom Perignon. That was how the house made its money. If the escort was able to make a little extra money with an assignation out the back, that was OK too.

A satisfied smile spread across Rupert's face as he remembered back to the first time he had suggested the "fantasy three." They were just so insistent that he would be contributing £100 's to their charity when, in practice, if someone waved half a lager at them around 10 p.m. on a Thursday night their resolve would disappear like the morning dew. Rupert wasn't really bothered about the money he didn't have to give; it was more about being right. If you said you thought something was going to happen and you didn't put some money where your mouth was you probably didn't mean it. You would be... well, an economist! It was something that people outside the industry didn't quite understand. They called him and his colleagues mercenary. Yes, there were plenty of greedy bastards in the industry who were solely interested in feathering their pockets without a care to the consequences. Calling a trader mercenary however, is like saying a baker is obsessed with bread." Of course I'm mercenary" he thought, my raw input is money, and my finished product is money. He treated the P and L more like a performance rating, or an exam mark, and if he was doing better than everyone else, he was happy. Having said that, he was aware that his privileged position meant that he could be a bit more laissez-faire about money than some of his colleagues, and one of the main reasons he strayed towards the rougher end of town when hiring traders was that he felt their hunger was greater.

With this Friday's fantasy three transferred to his mental "out-tray", he moved on to other matters in hand. When Regal Bank had set up the London operation, they asked Rupert to oversee the establishment of a Hong Kong branch too. When Charles "Chuck "Henderson III, the CEO of Regal Bank in the states had grandly outlined his plan, Rupert was reminded of the oft quoted phrase "two countries separated by a common tongue". Henderson's plans to "provide trading expertise 24/7 right around the planet", actually turned out to be two European traders in Hong Kong with a few Cantonese local hires backing them up. Regal Bank's impatience with the Hong Kong Stock Exchange meant that the traders were hired by Rupert in London and then flown out to Hong Kong to trade. Without proper employment visas they had to leave town every three months so they could come back in on tourist visas. Macau was used sometimes as a bolthole for the weekend. A 25 min Jetfoil ride would take them to a different jurisdiction where they would check into the Bela Vista and spend a couple of nights visiting one of the many Casinos located there. Other times they used their annual holidays to leave town, and on these occasions, cover from London for them had to be organised.

The business trip to Hong Kong was seen as a bit of a jolly. The relief trader would fly out a day or so before the Hong Kong trader was leaving for "handover". This made it sound like the relief trader would receive an in-depth briefing on positions/customer intentions and market stance from the Hong Kong trader. What it really meant was they could go for a night out together before the cover period started. Rupert had 4 US$ traders he could consider for the trip. John, Gary, Chopper and Alistair, a very safe pair of hands who ran the corporate book for him. Alistair had gone out to Hong Kong the last time, and although he would have been the most sensible choice, Rupert felt he had to give the chance to someone else. Gary was just too rough around the edges to send, and he could only imagine where Chopper could end up after a night on the sauce in

Wanchai. Fieldy it was then. He scribbled John's name in the 2.30 p.m. section of his desk diary as a reminder to tackle him about it and just as his mental "in-tray" was emptied the clarion call from Nicola, summoning the floor to the morning meeting brought him back to focus.

Like John, he was no great fan of the morning meeting. He rarely contributed, using the pretext that he didn't want to dictate opinion to the floor and would rather hear their views without prejudice. In truth he wasn't a great fan of public speaking at all. It was something he'd been forced to do at school but still avoided it unless absolutely necessary. Friday meetings were normally quite brief due to most people wanting to retire to the sanctuary of their desk and nurse their hangovers. Non-Farm Payroll Fridays were slightly different. On the first Friday of every month the U.S. Bureau of Labour Statistics released its Non-Farm Payroll numbers. They were considered the most important economic release for gauging the performance of the U.S. economy. Vince McDonell would normally hold forth on the implications of the numbers, the breakdown, the participation rate etc, etc. Today wasn't an NFP so he was mercifully brief. He did manage to squeeze in "crepuscular" though. Rupert's vocabulary was considerably wider than John's, but he still had no idea what on earth it meant.

The traditional New York, London, Tokyo clock display suspended from the ceiling of the trading floor ticked on to 03:01-08:01-16:01 and the phone boards started to light up with incoming calls. The traders picked up their blotters and commenced writing trades in. The system in the Eurobond market was head-to-head trading. Traders exchanged bid and offer prices with traders at other banks, and they could buy or sell as they wished on pre-agreed bid or offer levels and in universally accepted sizes. Strategy varied from house to house. Some traders were in the habit of not asking the issue they were really interested in for at least three or four prices as they thought this would lull the opposition into a false sense of security, others quite often had nothing to do but were press-ganged into asking as many prices as possible by their bosses so that they could ascertain exactly where the market was. Others were in a hurry to get rid of lots of one particular issue so would trade that issue right at the start of their run-through and then say something like "I've got lots of these to go mate, so I'll let you run if you want". What seemed like being reasonable with the opposition trader, giving him the chance to pass the position on before it tanked, was really blatant self-interest; the quicker he could get off that call and go and hit another unsuspecting trader the more he could get out of and at a good price.

Rupert was exempt from the everyday skirmishing. He had a book and positions of his own, but his book was termed an arbitrage book. His positions were aimed at a longer-term view and based upon relative value. He would also try to keep a weather eye on the total exposure of the floor and trade in the opposite direction if he felt they were risking too much. He could have got away with not having any positions at all, but he liked to have some skin in the game and felt he didn't watch markets properly unless he had some positions.

From time to time a trader would stand up and shout at the salespeople…" I've got some of these to go" …or" I'm looking for some of these" as they accumulated positions from their trading runs. The salespeople were expected to call their accounts, which varied from Investment Managers, Pension Funds, Central Banks, to Commercial Banks and various other institutions. Much like the brokers, good salespeople would know exactly what their accounts held and have a rough idea of where they wanted to sell it and what sort of stuff they would like to buy.

The babble of noise, punctuated by sporadic sudden outbursts, was comforting to Rupert and seemed to indicate to him a good level of business going on. His more cynical side wondered if a similar level of application would be apparent around bonus time in a couple of weeks.

Regal Bank's financial year ran from January to December and generally Rupert would send suggested numbers to head office for approval around the middle of the month of December when full year results were unlikely to change too much. The sign-off from New York would normally come back around the middle of January and then the "fireside chats" as the floor liked to call them would take place in his office. The week before bonuses was always identifiable by snatched chats in isolated corners of the floor as people speculated over what the pay-outs were going to be like and what they had heard. The period immediately after had a different dynamic. Some people may have organised themselves a new job and were waiting for the bonus cheque to clear before handing in their resignation, others would be mightily disappointed with their award and be stridently telling everyone else they were going to get another job, a select few would be practicing their "I'm not happy" face whilst being extremely smug about how much they were about to pick up. Bonus day itself would cast a strange pall over city workers as they keenly watched the internal extension lines for the call to summon them to the office. Lines would rarely ring more than once before being answered and some wags in the office would take delight in calling salespeople on the internal extensions just to see how quickly they pounced on the call.

As if on demand a dull thud on the desk in front of him announced the arrival in the internal post of a heavy brown cardboard envelope, emblazoned "Confidential" in red ink in several places. Scooping up the envelope with his coffee in the other hand he kicked himself back from the desk, got up, and headed for the refuge of his little-used office in the corner as he didn't want any prying eyes looking over his shoulder.

In his office he carefully unwound the string wrapped around a cardboard washer that kept the envelope shut and pulled out the contents. It contained New York's response to the numbers he had sent pre-Christmas. Generally, "Chuck" would not interfere too much with Rupert's suggestions, but there was always a bit of friction, counter-intuitively, over the lower-level awards. Rupert liked to give even the lesser performers on the floor a token at the end of the year. Chuck had a different take on things.

"Why you giving this guy ten grand?" Chuck would bark over the phone.

Rupert would counter with how helpful the guy had been or perhaps comment on his attitude but would normally be cut short by something like, "the guy's a loser and he's costing me money sitting there. If he's disappointed with his bone, then he can walk. Saves us paying him off, eh? You Brits gotta understand, we're in a meritocracy here! Listen Roop, cut a few of these ten grands from the losers and then if any of our top guys are disappointed, we can give it to them. That's commerce man."

Rupert would say goodbye with a sense of inevitability and wondered whether, in a little dig at Chuck he should start putting Rupert "roop" De Villiers on his business cards. On reflection he decided that Chuck would just think Rupert was finally "getting with the program" and the inferred dig would fly way over his head.

On opening the envelope, a quick scan confirmed his suspicions. Five or six names had a red pen struck through them with a "o" next to them and the bottom line had been adjusted to the lower amount. It would leave him a bit of wriggle room if anyone cut up rough about their award, but he was pretty sure he could justify what he was giving to most of his people. He fished for his Mont Blanc fountain pen in the inner pocket of his jacket and signed with a flourish at the bottom of the page. After blowing on the wet ink for five seconds he slipped it back into the envelope, re-wrapped the string and took it to the door of his office where he summoned Sid the postman and handed it to him personally. This wasn't something to be left in the post tray for inquisitive eyes to be tempted by.

From his standing position, leaning against the doorjamb of his office he had a perfect view of the back of Chloe as she bent over the desk, gathering in tickets as they spat out of the end of the conveyor belt. He knew everyone called her a dumb blonde, but he had danced with her a couple of times at the company Christmas bash and had felt electrified when their hips touched during one of the slower tunes. He could still remember the smell of her now as he lasciviously tried to imagine how she would look naked. She had disappeared after the second dance to go and do shots with some of the settlements guys and Rupert felt his position meant he shouldn't go chasing her, but he desperately wanted to get to know her better. He was due at his parents' palatial estate in Leicestershire for a shooting party on the weekend, where his mother would wheel another selection of pearl necklace clad debutantes past him in the vain hope of Rupert finding "a suitable match". How he wished he could swap Leicestershire for a dirty weekend in Romford. With an almost audible sigh Rupert headed back to his trading desk. Somehow, he would have to make it happen. His mental "in-tray" now had only one outstanding task.

CHAPTER 5

A cross the City, Frank Robinson was pouring himself out of a taxi. He felt "pouring" was the right word as he was pretty sure the majority of his body was still liquid from the night before. He was hoping the two smoked salmon bagels he'd picked up might redress the balance. Even for Frank, Thursday night had been excessive. Getting himself out of bed had been a gargantuan struggle and were it not for the two pinches of cocaine he'd quickly snorted before getting dressed he would probably still be there now. He glanced up at the large, illuminated lettering on the outside of his building. "Central Brokers" the red sign proclaimed. Robbo hustled in through the main entrance and went through to the back of the building where his plan was to take the service elevator up to his floor and sidle into his seat, which was very close to that entrance, without too much fuss. After prodding the "up "button two or three times the doors drew back to reveal a wiry old woman in a blue tabard with a mop and bucket and the African security guard who Robbo normally saw at duty on the reception desk. With a brief nod of recognition, Robbo squeezed his not inconsiderable frame in beside them and pushed the button for his floor. Had he been able to see behind him he would have noticed the guard and the cleaner with their hands over their noses, trying to blot out the brewery like smell his whole body was emanating, but Robbo's senses were anything but acute at that moment and as the lift door opened all his efforts were concentrated on opening the fire exit door as quietly as possible. He needn't have bothered. The cacophony that greeted him as soon as he edged into the room told him that he had used this route one too many times on a Friday morning. A standing ovation from most of his colleagues, and some wise guy blowing a train whistle they'd nicked from a guard on a trip to Royal Ascot meant nobody missed his arrival at work that morning. "Very fucking funny!" was his imaginative reply. "you'se lot clapping like a fucking pack of seals, must mean Plummer's brokers are all on the line doing the biz!".

Frank plonked down on his chair and without taking his jacket off picked a handset up and started talking. He was shouting through the box to Fieldy and would continue until the hubbub died down even if Fieldy didn't answer. He liked the banter really and would have been one of the worst critics of anyone had the roles been reversed, but he also wanted to establish the perception that when he was in late it was because of the time and effort he had committed the night before into establishing profitable relationships with traders...when other people were late, they were "just out on the piss". The fact that the traders he was courting had normally left halfway through the evening was merely academic.

As his colleagues gradually settled back into their routines, he awkwardly slipped his jacket off arm by arm without standing up and slipped over the back of his seat. Reaching into the inside pocket his fingers first hit the small empty polythene bag that still had some small traces of white powder in. He decided to leave that for the moment and after delving a bit further he came up with two wrinkled receipts. Looking at the details of the previous night's extravagances did engender just the merest trace of guilt in Robbo, but the pang was a fleeting one. He resolved to make his next call in to the trader with whom he had started the evening off with. Although a direct link between entertainment and writing some tickets was not specifically mentioned, most traders were smart enough to know the broker wasn't taking them out and buying them Kobe Beef and bottles of Haut Brion because they liked their company. In his time Frank had sat through all sorts of evenings listening to what traders wanted to expound upon; from tiling the upstairs bathroom to another one's obsession with tropical fish. Broking technique was to take note of a trader's interest, football or rugby for instance so that if an event came up that would really be interesting to them such as a big European game or an England International at Twickenham, they would be invited, for which they would show financial appreciation. The opportunities for entertainment in the wall-tiling and tropical fish arenas were somewhat limited. In cases like this, Frank would revert to the lowest common denominator. On any evening out, where the conversation was floundering due to Frank's inability to distinguish between a Guppy and an Angel Fish, he would suggest going on to a strip bar. "Everyone likes a bird, don't they?"

If Frank were being honest with himself, the normal outcome would be for the trader to be a bit embarrassed by the whole thing and make his excuses early after arrival at one of Frank's regular haunts. Frank would then reason with himself that it would be a shame to waste the night now he'd made the effort to get there, and his departure would be significantly later than that of the trader.

Frank was rarely honest with himself. If he was capable of being honest with himself, he might have reached the conclusion that the stripper he had started seeing was perhaps not that interested in his corpulent figure and unkempt look of a 32 year old City worker and maybe realise that the £10 notes he was in the regular habit of stuffing into her bikini bottoms could have had something to do with it. He set great store by the fact she had revealed to him that her real name was not actually "Ferrari, but "Ana" and she came from Portugal. He first met her in Blues, a large pub on the borders of the City where there was a stage for a stripper to perform her act whilst some of her companions would wander through the watching punters with a pint glass collecting contributions in anticipation of their own stage shows. Experienced performers could distinguish between the sound of pound coins hitting their glass and random silver thrown in there without even looking, and punters who put in anything that needed to be folded up were given special treatment. He thought she was stunning the first time he saw her and after dropping the £5 note in her glass she seemed very friendly. When she got up to do her first dance Frank thought he had never seen a body so mesmerizing, and the fact that she didn't seem to take her eyes off him throughout the whole dance was especially attractive to him. When he left the pub that lunchtime his whole focus was on finding an excuse to get back there as soon as possible. He would perhaps have been surprised to know that Ana was very focused during the dance too. The front door lock of her flat had been sticking and she needed a locksmith, the front door also needed painting. In fact, there was a paint shop just up the road... she would go when her set was over. "It's not my fault if deep smouldering gazes are misinterpreted by punters. I'm just good at my job", concluded Ana.

As the morning wore on the effects of Robbo's morning "pick-me-up" wore off. He either needed one more to keep him going or a couple of swift pints in a nearby boozer. He'd have headed down to Blues if Ana was going to be there, but she wasn't working that day. He pressed the Regal Bank line and moved his mouth close to the microphone "Fieldy, fancy a quick steak down Bangers?"

Bangers was one of a chain of Davy's wine houses in the City. Davy's was a bona fide wine merchant with restaurant outlets that did pretty respectable steaks. They served "Davy's Old Wallop", a bitter that tasted a bit like washing up water to Robbo but when served in a pewter mug as they did and combined with sawdust strewn across the floor and random Port barrels to perch around, the atmosphere was redolent of 18th Century London. All that was missing was some men in powdered wigs sucking on thin-stemmed pipes.

"You're done Shag" came the reply from the speaker box. "See you at 12.01".

Robbo made sure he was down there at noon so as he could have two mugs of "Old Wallop" set up. Like many City eateries, Bangers was a sub-terranean establishment. The sort you emerged from after a three-hour lunch to be dazzled by the fact the sun was still out. The sound of Fieldy's distinctive steel tips on the stairs down to the bar announced his arrival, accompanied by a friend.

"Chopper was at a loose end, so I brought him along" said John, with no hint of apology.

"Yeah, yeah, no problem mate...how are you, Chopper? What you want to drink?"

"I'm good son. I'll have a Rotterdam" replied Chopper.

Robbo turned to scan the bar, searching for clues as to what Chopper actually wanted to drink, but could see nothing apart from the solitary "Old Wallop "hand pump and a soft drinks dispenser. Although he was quite used to Chopper, it was very early in the day for him to have become unintelligible.

"What's a Rotterdam then? He reluctantly asked.

"A large port son!" Chopper cackled, delighted with this new addition to his "mockney slang" vocabulary. Robbo just resignedly wondered how this lunch was going to end if Chopper was starting it all off with a large Port.

With their drinks in hand, they left the bar and wandered further through into the bowels of the City to take their table.

Against Robbo's expectations, and by City standards, the lunch was a relatively modest one. John mentioned he wanted to keep half sober as he was seeing Rupert in the afternoon about a trip to Hong Kong. Rupert would think he was surprising John with this news, but you could always find out what was going on in banks by being friendly with the secretaries. They typed everything and booked all the appointments and could be remarkably talkative after a few glasses of Laurent Perrier Rose. As John shared this information with the table, he adopted a sort of world-weary "I have to go to Hong Kong soon, could do without it" stance, trying to mask the fact that he was tremendously excited about what would be his first foreign business trip and the Business Class travel that he felt a man like himself should always enjoy. The only conversation of any sincerity in the whole lunch occurred when Chopper left the table briefly to go to the gents. As soon as he was out of earshot Robbo leaned forward across the table. "You got any gear on you mate?"

John's head span one way and then the other checking Chopper had actually left.

"Nah, trying to be good this month" he replied. "You tried Delroy?"

Robbo swallowed another half glass of red wine before answering. "He weren't at his usual spot today".

John smiled a knowing smile. "You ain't got to worry about that no more. The flash bastard's had one of them car phones put in his cab. You can call him!". John flicked a business card with the details across the table. "It's just like ordering pizzas now!"

CHAPTER 6

Delroy rubbed his hands together as he surveyed the snow falling outside his cab. He was tempted to breathe on them but decided that if the woolly gloves he was wearing weren't doing the job, then a bit of blowing probably wasn't going to make that much difference. His white cab driver mates all attributed his apparent cold bloodedness to his West Indian heritage. Delroy couldn't be bothered to tell them that the hospital in Bethnal Green where he was born was probably no nearer to the equator than their own birthplaces. He was pretty sure of the reason he dressed up like this to drive a cab, and it was almost certainly the central heating in his council flat. He actually paid for it now that he owned the place, but having got used to lounging around in a t-shirt and boxers he thought it was an extravagance worth continuing. He was parked in a marked-out bay in London Wall. There were many spaces around the City where cabs could stop and park for free. These were in addition to the ranks outside stations where you could wait for business as commuters flocked out. The business that Delroy would park up and wait for, meant he preferred the parking spots to the ranks. He leaned forward and checked the hidden compartment under his dashboard. He usually had a good supply on Fridays as his customers had normally binged a fair bit on their Thursday night excursions and the thought of lasting a whole weekend away from their desks (and their supplier) meant they often felt the need to stockpile some to carry them over. He hoped they wouldn't be too put off by the cold snap, but was reasonably confident that demand was constant, come rain or shine.

As he was prone to do, with time on his hands, his mind drifted to well-trodden philosophical ground. Could he justify what he did? Drugs were the Devil's creation in his mother's lectures, and she also included alcohol in this category. That was probably the reason Reginald needed to go down to his garage to drink rum and play dominoes with his mates. Growing up, his first experience of drugs was the commonplace use of marijuana, or Ganja, at parties attended by his family's circle of friends who were predominantly Caribbean. As he got older, and talked to people more about it, he realised the cultural importance it had to Jamaicans in particular. The colours of the flag were supposed to represent the people, the sun, and the abundant agricultural riches. Anyone Jamaican you asked would tell you the green was for the "'erb". Delroy had never smoked, so really didn't enjoy pulling on some huge spliff when they were passed around and preferred sipping on a can of Carlsberg Special Brew. He did question from time to time how different the world might have been if Sir Walter Raleigh had brought back cannabis leaves rather than tobacco. Would everyone have been too zonked out for a couple of World Wars? Would people illicitly sneak tobacco into the country and would the government willingly take massive tax revenue from the companies that marketed cannabis whilst cracking down on anyone who fancied a sneaky Old Holborn?

Delroy's treatise on cannabis versus tobacco had reached an hypothetical dead-end so his mind passed to cocaine. Ganja was a natural product in his mind as opposed to cocaine being a pharmaceutical product. If people can take aspirin, why can't they take coke? Is alcohol not a drug? He wondered to himself what the criteria were for governments to sanction one product and ban another. "Money" he guessed. As far as he knew cocaine was related to morphine and they used that all the time in hospitals. He decided, as he had many times before, that he didn't have enough information to follow this argument through to a satisfactory conclusion so he would fall back on two old friends.

a) If people wanted something badly enough, they'd get it somewhere.
b) If someone's going to make money on it, may as well be me.

It was not philanthropy on Delroy's part, but simple business sense to do his utmost to ensure the supply he was marketing was of good quality. Dead customers were not good for business. This led him to a further thought. Perhaps there should be no restraints on any drugs.... people stupid enough to overdo it would kill themselves... wasn't this some sort of Darwinian "survival of the fittest"?

His dystopian vision of a potential future was interrupted by an as yet unfamiliar electronic burbling informing him that his new car phone was ringing.

"Hello, DJ here." He resisted the temptation to say "in my cab" because he guessed whoever was calling him on that number would have known that by now.

"Hi Delroy, it's Robbo, you nearby?" the line was very poor, but Delroy still marvelled at the near "Star Trek" technology that made it possible to talk to people in his cab.

"Well, it depends where you are!" teased Delroy.

"I'm in a call box in Elwood Street".

"I'll pick you up in two minutes". He sought the button to end the call, remembering this type of phone didn't hang up when you put it back in the cradle, then placed the handset down and used both hands to pull on the heavy steering wheel to execute a complete U-turn across London Wall and head down to Elwood Street.

Robbo stepped into the cab almost before it stopped moving and they were quickly off again in the direction of Bishopsgate.

"Afternoon guvnor" said Delroy affecting an exaggerated east-end accent. "What can I do for you?"

"I'll have a ton's worth mate" said Robbo as he perched on one of the fold-down seats backing onto the driver. They were known in the City as the brokers' seats as usually the traders would be allowed to sit in the comfier back seats on any journey.

Robbo slipped five £20 notes through the small gap in the glass division between himself and Delroy as the cab was navigated across Bishopsgate and into Devonshire Row. It was a dead-end road with a turning circle at its end. They pulled up outside one of the entrances to Devonshire Square and as Robbo got out, he put his head through the open passenger side window as if to pay for his ride. "Your change Sir, you want a receipt?" Delroy smiled as he handed over the small powder filled bags and watched Robbo stuff them inside his jacket.

"No, you're alright thanks Delroy, you gave me a whole book of them last time! Have a good weekend". Robbo quickly stomped off through the snow to the shelter of the nearest building.

As he watched Robbo's large figure disappearing in his rear-view mirror Delroy recalled how he had begun supplying cocaine to Robbo, Grub and their immediate circle of city workers.

A late-night fare from the West End a couple of years ago, and an overheard conversation between Grub and a colleague had ended with Delroy saying, "you know I could get you all the Charlie you want much cheaper than that".

"Yeah, but is it any good?" Grub questioned.

"Well, my mate Andy don't get any complaints! How about I get you a sample?"

"Do you live here? Delroy pointed up at the large, terraced house Grub had directed him to. "What time you leave for work?"

"What's this, 20 fucking questions?" said Grub aggressively through the cab's open passenger side window.

"No, I'll pick you up for work on the way in and you can sample the goods if you want." Delroy rejoined patiently.

"Alright, you're done. 7.00 Thursday morning" agreed Grub.

As Grub made his way up the small flight of stairs to his front door Delroy shouted out of his still open window as he pulled away from the kerb.

"And don't worry, I won't charge you for the fare in!"

CHAPTER 7

A ndy O'Brien tried to make the last few punches really count. As sweat dripped from his close-cropped hair into his eyes he imagined the heavy leather covered punch bag to be one of his many enemies and rained blows down on it, making sure not to lose technique in his frenzy. He was getting better at controlling and focusing his anger and his trainer had recently commented that he could go a long way if he turned pro. Andy wasn't interested in the exposure, or the discipline required to be honest, and his favourite fighting move, the headbutt, was definitely not within the Marquess of Queensberry rules, but he still harboured a sneaking desire to pit himself against others to prove his dominance. Picking up his towel he headed for the showers. In keeping with the martial theme of the gym the showers were spartan to say the least. Andy could have afforded a more upmarket gym easily, but somehow it seemed more fitting to him to deny himself luxuries when training to fight. He did allow himself the indulgence of a splash of Halston Z14 though. He liked to smell good.

Feeling alive and fresh he walked out of the gym into the bustle of Hoxton market. Stalls selling fruit and veg, and household wares made up most of the vendors, as housewives in head scarves milled around searching out bargains. Occasional shouts from the stallholders punctuated the ever-present soundtrack of one stall holder playing his pirated cassettes on a huge boom-box suspended from one of the top slats of his stall.

The council flats behind the market were his destination. He had always lived there, and elements of his large, Irish descended family were dotted around all over the place. It was impossible for him to feel threatened around here. From time-to-time people would nod and acknowledge him as he walked along, but few held his eyes for long. Over the last few years, he had established himself as the alpha male in the area and the hub of most of the criminal activities. Andy was uneducated but not stupid. He knew his position was one that had to be constantly maintained. Anybody "taking the piss" had to be swiftly and viciously dealt with to make sure the message was reinforced regularly, "It doesn't pay to fuck with Andy O'Brien". It helped that in the East End, the majority of people looked upon the police as the enemy. The Met had a policy of putting PCs into the area that came from out of London. Preferably from a hard town up North, where there was no risk of any familial ties or school age relationships that could be used to influence them to be lenient. This usually meant from Glasgow or

Liverpool and only served to poison relationships with the worthies of the East End even more. Some of them had been known to descend upon teenagers who were deemed "troublemakers" and pile them into the back of their Black Marias (or meat wagons as they were known) for a good kicking, as if this was some form of future crime prevention. Incidents like that meant the last thing anyone around his area were going to do was "grass" on Andy to the police. In fact, it had happened once, and the grass's name had been daubed all over the flats soon after. He was hastily moved into a witness protection programme out of London. The case subsequently collapsed as he changed his testimony, but he could still never return.

As Andy passed the Green Man at the end of the market, a regular watering hole of his, he was instantly reminded of a similar day three years ago when he saw a figure detach himself from the lamppost he'd been leaning against and head towards him.

In a smooth motion Andy slipped his gym bag from his shoulder and into his left hand freeing up his right hand for action. The man approaching also made ready, his right hand coming out of the pocket of his track-suit bottoms and projecting towards Andy.

"Top of the morning to you Paddy!" Delroy clasped Andy's outstretched hand with a large smile and in return Andy attempted a Jamaican "waya a say bredren?" Four words of Patois were Andy's limit and he lapsed back into his normal growl. "What's going on Delboy?"

Andy had started using Delboy rather than Delroy not long after the "Only Fools and Horses "series had started on TV. He thought it was a great nick name for his mate who was always searching around for the next get rich quick scheme and suspected that was the reason for this encounter. His first contact with Delroy had been a fight when they were teenagers. He couldn't even remember the reason for it, but he had flown at Delroy with flailing fists. Surprised to have missed with his first couple of shots he had been wrestled to the ground and before he knew what was happening the heavier boy was sitting on him, knees on his shoulders, unable to move. Aware of his vulnerability he had launched into a ferocious tirade. "I'm gonna ram a fucking bottle down your neck, do you know who I am?"

Andy hoped the reputation of his brothers and uncles would be enough to make Delroy think twice before the inevitable crunch of blows upon his face.

Delroy looked down upon him, trying to reinforce his superiority by showing a complete lack of concern for the threats he was hearing "ya chat fuckery white boy".

Despite the gang that Delroy ran with at the time and the general dog eat dog nature of his life, he found no great desire to escalate things and when Andy's companion said, "come away Andy, just leave him", Delroy dismounted and allowed his assailant to get up and leave the scene. Delroy always wondered if things would have turned out different if there were not a couple of his gang there with him but that was all academic. When he found out Andy's reputation, he thanked his lucky stars he had not inflicted any damage upon him. A visit from the O'Brien boys would not have left his mum's flat in a great state of repair, let alone his body. Their next encounter was not for four years. Doing the knowledge meant getting a moped and riding around all the routes to familiarise yourself with London, and it was on his return from one of these journeys, late at night, that he saw a couple of hooded men chasing another guy down a darkened street near his home. The second and slightly heavier of the two chasing guys was wielding a long-handled axe and Delroy couldn't see any trees. To this day he still wonders what sudden impulse made him do it, but without slowing down he headed straight for him, tilting the moped onto its side and simultaneously jumping off leaving the speeding moped to continue its progress into the legs of the axeman. The high-pitched scream told him he'd found his target and the axe span away into the air. He turned around to see the other hooded man on the receiving end of a flurry of punches from the heavily muscled man he had been chasing. The final blow of the combination was a head-jolting uppercut, sending the man's head jerking back. Delroy thought that if that blow didn't kill him then the impact as his head hit the concrete of the road surely would. Almost before that happened the hunted man had sprinted over to the grounded moped and picked up the fallen axe.

"You aint gonna kill him are you mate?" Delroy incredulously asked as the man stood over the moaning assailant and drew the axe back over his head.

His answer was a swift downward blow across the hooded man's knee, separating his lower leg cleanly and making a dent in the moped laying beneath.

"Nah, but I got to send a message. Pick your moped up and get it away from here. The Old Bill will be all over the place soon". As Delroy got his first look at the man's face, he realised who it was, and reached up to the chin strap of his helmet, undid it and lifted it off.

"You remember me?" Delroy stood there looking into his eyes.

"Fuck me. Wondered when I'd bump into you again". Andy had the beginnings of a smile curling around his lips." Why did you do that then?".

"Didn't know it was you, did I? All you white blokes look the same!"

Delroy walked over to his moped and Andy helped him shift the unconscious man's body so that they could stand it up and wheel it to his nearby garage. The wail of police sirens in the distance suggested they were not a minute too soon. As he locked the garage door Andy turned to him and shook him firmly by the hand. "Don't worry about the moped, I'll replace it, and don't say a word to anyone about this to anyone, ok?"

"Remember, I owe you big time...I'll be in touch".

In two days, Delroy answered the door to two of Andy's associates, "Mr Joseph? Here's the moped keys you asked for".

Delroy's quizzical look prompted them to elaborate.

"It's in your garage" they explained.

"How the fuck did you get in there?" asked Delroy.

The elder of the two men had a thick Irish accent "Sure now, if I were you, I'd get a new lock for that garage sir. Only had to fecking blow on it to open it! Have a nice day now!"

With that they turned on their heels and made for the lifts.

Delroy had been impressed with his new moped and the fact that Andy was as good as his word. Their subsequent meetings had been sporadic, but their relationship was now on a very familiar footing, and they had a good deal of mutual respect. For this reason, Andy knew that Delroy must want something if he'd made the effort to wait outside his gym for him on a cold morning.

"I guess you want to have a chat about something?" said Andy, feigning a sort of "what now?" face when in truth he was more than happy to do Delroy a few favours. The scrape he'd been rescued from that night with the moped had been a seminal event in his rise to the top.

"I'm going for some pie and mash; you want to come with me?"

"Yeah lovely, two horse meat pies and a pile of lumpy mash with green shit all over it! No thanks, but I'll take a mug of tea while you eat yours".

"They do jellied eels too!" teased Andy, knowing they were even lower down on Delroy's list. The two old friends both chuckled and headed towards Cooke's.

As Andy wolfed down his pies, Delroy explained that he had a potential buyer of the high-grade cocaine that he knew Andy was involved in and wondered how hard it would be for Andy to send some his way when needed. A plan was worked out and without any negotiation Andy told Delroy he would give it to him at cost, which whilst it pleased Delroy, pleased Andy more. He hated being in someone's debt and much preferred people to owe him favours that he could call on when needed. That was always the way he worked with the bent cops he paid. Give them something up front and they are hooked.

From then on, Delroy, with the help of Grub, developed quite a few City clients and the purpose of his regular meetings with Andy became twofold. He would pay for the last consignment and tell Andy how much he wanted in the next one, which would mysteriously turn up in his garage a couple of days after their meetings. He had upgraded the lock on his garage now, but Andy's men found it easy to access it with the new key he'd had copied for them. Andy never tired of telling him as his demands rose "At this rate, and the margin you're probably taking on it, this time next year you _will_ be a millionaire Delboy!"

CHAPTER 8

B onus day had finally arrived at Regal Bank. The hopes and fears of its employees would be laid bare today and the end result would be the same in most cases, whether good or bad...retire to a nearby bar for the post-match analysis and comparisons. Rupert fervently hoped that people would not discuss their awards but was realistic enough to know that somehow, everybody knew what everyone else earned in this place and similarly everyone knew who got what in the bonus round. He had no idea why people should discuss it, and guessed there was always a bit of leakage from people who worked in personnel and saw all the numbers. There were so many inter-office romances going on in that place that there must be a bit of pillow talk.

The pile of A4 sized white envelopes that had been deposited on his desk by Sid the postman sat silently, accusingly, prompting him to get started with the task. He had ducked out of the morning meeting and could feel the eyes of the room on him through the glass walls of his office. His title was Head of Trading, but as the Head of Sales had recently been hired by a competing firm, he currently had responsibility for the sales staff too. Rupert would have preferred to get all the people to whom he was going to give bad news in first, but realised avid watchers would soon start predicting who was getting nothing and he didn't want that. Alphabetical order was the best standby and as he drained the last drop of his coffee and threw the cardboard cup cleanly into the wastepaper bin on the other side of his desk, he looked up the internal extension number for Nicola Avery. He punched the numbers in and as expected the call was picked up on its first ring.

"Good morning, Nicola Avery" announced the cheerful voice in his ear.

"Hi Nic, it's Rupert. Can you come and see me please?". He replaced the receiver without waiting for a reply and picked up the first envelope from the pile. He knew the contents of this letter would make many of the salespeople on the floor very happy, and also that it would be of very little consequence to Nicola as her family were "minted" as Gary Davis liked to say. He couldn't see how someone's private wealth made any difference to the reward they deserved for a good year's work, and he was pretty sure Nicola would hardly look at the actual number on the letter and she would still show effusive gratitude and enthusiasm for the job. This first fireside chat was going to be relatively easy but there were more troublesome ones to come.

As the morning passed, Rupert had adopted a new tactic to stop the spoof calls to people's internal numbers from mischievous colleagues. He just told whoever he saw to tap the shoulder of the next name on the list and ask them to come to his office. It meant he didn't get a break, but that suited him as he wanted it finished as quickly as possible. Some people amused him, going back to their desks and using a calculator to work out how much tax they would lose from their bonuses. "What are you doing in this business if you can't work out 60% in your head?" he thought to himself. "Thank God the top rate of tax isn't 83% like it was before Maggie! "In principle, Rupert was opposed to anything above 50%. Working and giving away more than you got yourself just didn't seem right to him, but as a famous man once wrote, "nothing can be said to be certain except death and taxes".

By around 10.45 a.m. Rupert was all done and ventured out of his office on to the trading floor to sample the atmosphere. Noise levels were not quite back to normal, but the pregnant silence of the earlier morning had thankfully disappeared. He wandered around the floor and stood behind John Field's chair. "Much going on Fieldy?"

"Bits and pieces boss. I managed to get shot of those EIB's I got slotted in last night. That bird at SocGen Paris always makes shit prices first thing in the morning! The problem is getting into her first. It's like trying to book a GP's appointment; there's so many people ringing her at 08.01!"

"Haha, good stuff John, you doing anything for lunch?" enquired Rupert.

"Me and Gazza are going down that antique shop in Leadenhall market. Got a few bob to throw at some furniture today. "Fieldy's unsubtle reply was loud enough for at least four of his colleagues who had received nothing in the bonus chats to hear. If it were possible, their opinion of John Field took another step lower.

Rupert continued further around the horseshoe of desks and came to a stop behind Nicola. She seemed unaware of his presence and was totally consumed in tapping away at a keyboard connected to a stand-alone screen which was sitting on the unoccupied desk next to her. Unlike all the other screens dotted around the trading floor this one had orange text rather than the hi-vis green that was standard issue. Nicola had requested a Bloomberg system last year and her logic appealed to Rupert. Bloomberg had started as an in-house system for Merril Lynch to manage and analyse their trading. The system was so good that there was a split at Merril's as some of the management thought they should keep it as a massive analytical advantage over their competitors, whilst others thought that they should sell it whilst it was comparatively unique. The latter group won the day and by 1986 terminals were popping up on the desks of the more informed trading houses in New York and London. Nicola used it for relative value analysis with which she could persuade clients of the value of certain investments that she was marketing. More importantly, in Rupert's mind, she also made it available to the traders, who while they didn't like to admit it, used her research to position certain issues. Nicola was smart, attractive, from a rich family, and always happy. Rupert still couldn't work out why he didn't have feelings for her but as his gaze shifted to the end of the horseshoe, and lighted upon Chloe he guessed she might be a contributory factor. Although she didn't report to him directly, he had taken it upon himself to make sure her back-office boss gave her a nice bonus. She was very efficient, but in truth Rupert was planning to let her know what he had done and hopefully ingratiate himself a bit further with her. Perhaps he should see what she was doing for lunch? He left Nicola earnestly typing and sauntered up to Chloe who was fussily checking her shock of blonde hair in a small mirror.

"Quiet today then Chloe?" asked Rupert as she looked around.

"Yes boss, aint seen a ticket for a good half-hour. All these lazy bastards got their money and downed tools I reckon!"

Rupert's brow furrowed slightly at this. He was sure he'd heard some trades being done whilst he was having his firesides and he'd definitely seen a few since he came out. Even as he was standing there he heard Gazza shout at a salesman "Ok, 2 million yours at 98". He watched as the salesman filled in the details on a pink "SELL" ticket and throw it into the conveyor belt system above his desk.

The ticket began its journey around to Chloe's input desk but mysteriously, after sufficient time had elapsed, was nowhere to be seen. Rupert walked back towards the nearest bend in the system to Chloe. A tangled mass of blue and pink slips had somehow got stuck there and nothing could make its way past. Rupert fished a handful out and brandished them in the air. "Er Chloe" he shouted across the floor, loud enough for not just her to hear.

Chloe's reply, although not purposely loud, was raucous enough for the whole room to hear.

"Fuck me, I better get my arse in gear!". She slipped on the white high-heeled court shoes that normally resided at the foot of her desk and tottered up to where Rupert was still holding some tickets.

"Well don't just stand there! Give us an 'and" she rebuked him and leant forward over the desk at full stretch to recover some more tickets. Rupert stood transfixed for a while admiring the shape of her from behind before realising it was probably obvious to most people in the room what was on his mind. He tore his gaze away from her and caught Nicola's eye on the way. For once she was not staring at her screen and if perhaps he was a little more perceptive, he would have sensed something in her eyes. A mixture of accusation and sadness maybe. Chloe's faux pas did not go unnoticed and some of the traders made the effort to stand up and offer some opinions to her. "If your brains was dynamite, you wouldn't have enough to blow your fucking head off!" was Fieldy's contribution. She simply turned and gave him the finger in response as she took the tickets back to her desk. One thing was for sure, Chloe was not going to be free for lunch now. He deposited the tickets in his hand at Chloe's desk and retreated to the refuge of his office.

At 12.01 p.m. Gary Davis and John Field met at the coat hooks around the outside of the trading floor and prepared to brave the outside world. John wanted to brief Gary on his role for today's antique buying expedition which he had reluctantly agreed to accompany him on.

"All I want you to do Gazza is stand there and look like you know a bit about old furniture".

"What sort of look is that then?" asked Gary.

"Well for a start, I could do without you wearing that Arthur Daley camel coat."

"Bollocks to that, it's cold out there. What's your plan?" asked Gary.

"Well, I've seen a nice chest of drawers down this shop in Leadenhall Market, and I want to get it. You know what these places are like. All the prices are ramped up because we're City Faces. I'm going to tell him you're an expert and bid him about 30% less and I bet he'll still bite my hand off!"

"Sounds simple enough, and lunch in Bolton's afterwards, yes?"

"Done" said John as he shrugged his trench coat onto his shoulders and marched towards the lifts.

In ten minutes, they were outside a Dickensian looking shop with various bric-a-brac and furniture in the window and as John opened the door, a reassuringly solid "clang "came from the old-fashioned bell on a coiled spring above the door. A noise from the back of the shop heralded the arrival of a character that fitted in perfectly with the décor of the shop. He was balding, dressed in a waistcoat with a crisp white shirt and bowtie underneath, and wore a pair of half-moon glasses. As he shuffled across the polished floorboards of the shop, he tugged on a watch-chain on his waistcoat and hauled out a well-used fob watch. There was a pause, as he verified whether it was past noon or not, before he greeted them. "Good afternoon gentlemen. How may I be of assistance?"

In a business-like manner John stomped across to an item of furniture in the window of the shop. There was a small cardboard tag tied to one of the knobs with "6140" written in pencil on it.

"I'm interested in this chest of drawers here." John tapped on it as he spoke. "My mate here is an antiques expert and insists it's not worth a penny over four grand. I can pay cash too if you want. What do you say?" John was sure people of this ilk weren't used to high level negotiation like him and he was waiting for the guy's comeback before mercilessly forcing him down to the price.

The elderly shop assistant made his way over to the piece and carefully bent down to study the tag for a moment then straightened up, pushed the glasses back up his nose, and addressed his customer.

"6140 is actually the catalogue number Sir, the Bureau (he stressed Bureau as chest of drawers was a far too workaday description for the charming mahogany writing desk in his estimation), is actually priced at £430".

The heavy tick-tock of a nearby Grandfather clock was all that could be heard for a second or two as the information was processed by an open-mouthed Fieldy.

"Would Sir like it delivered?" followed up the assistant, with only the merest hint of sarcasm.

John could sense Gazza starting to lose it behind him and was sure he could sense a little smug grin creeping across the shop assistant's face. John swiftly span on his heels, dragged a handful of Gary's camel coat and propelled him towards the door.

"I don't want it if it's a fucking fake" he snarled as his parting comment and slammed the door back pushing Gary out in front of him.

It was only mid-way through their second course at Bolton's before Gary stopped laughing.

CHAPTER 9

With Bonus Day out of the way most institutions in the City settled back into the rhythm of getting their heads down to make money in what was usually one of the two most profitable periods of the year. It was important to get a good start to the year and have something in reserve for when holidays started. The second period to make money was September to November. After Thanksgiving everyone would be celebrating Christmas for a month. It was the beginning of March and Fieldy was still doing well and looked upon his upcoming trip to Hong Kong as a good chance to take stock of things, and also rack up a decent amount of entertainment on the Bank's American Express card. He had been fully equipped for the trip by Madelaine Cooper, Rupert's amazingly efficient p.a.

As requested, she had handed him his tickets, joined the BA executive club for him on his behalf, sorted his Hong Kong dollars in a thick transparent envelope and given him a print-out of his hotel reservation. "Will you need a map to find the office John?" she had asked him as she handed over his travel pack?

John bit his tongue on the sarcastic response he would have given to any other woman on the trading floor. Somehow, although she was only a few years older than him, she projected a kind of maternal strictness that John felt a little bit intimidating.

"Nah, you're alright Madelaine. I'll ask at the hotel. How do I get to Heathrow?"

"Well, If I were you, for a 9 p.m. flight I would take the tube, but alternatively I could arrange a car, or you can organise that yourself. You may want to book the return with the same company. Just make sure you keep the receipts." Madelaine spun on her heel and headed back to her desk.

For John, there was no way he was risking his newly bought "executive" luggage on public transport with every other Tom, Dick and Harry at rush hour. He knew just the man to drive him to the airport. He sorted through the dog-eared cards in his wallet and placed one on his desk. "DJ's Taxi Service" it proclaimed in garish purple lettering. Underneath, in a more sober black font was added "Airport transfers and bookings...call me on my car phone" followed by the number.

John carefully punched in the numbers and heard the ringing tone.

In two rings the familiar tone of Delroy answered. "Hello, DJ here"

John could just about hear him above a thumping bass line. "Can you turn that down?" John bellowed into his handset.

"Chill mate, Frankie Beverley was just getting to the good bit".

As if to emphasise this, Delroy stopped talking and sung along for two lines to the music (now at a much lower volume in the background) # Joy and Pain, like sunshine, and rain#

"What's that shit? Give me a bit of Madness any day," said John. "Listen I've got a job for you. You interested?"

"How many bags you want?"

"Shh Shh! Don't you know these lines are taped?" warned John, instinctively dropping his voice and standing to turn away from any prying ears on the desk.

"I need to go to Heathrow Monday next week. You want the fare?" he asked.

"What time?" crackled Delroy's voice back.

"It's a 9 p.m. flight so I guess about 5 p.m. It would be nice to get there and enjoy the benefits of the business lounge for a while". John's voice had regained its normal volume and unlike his earlier comments, he wanted everyone around to hear him now.

"There'll be a lot of traffic around then", the cab driver's cautionary voice seemed anything but keen for what John considered a nice little earner.

"Fuck me, you're a cabbie aint you?" John was incredulous.

"Alright, alright.... calm down mate. I'll see you outside the office on Monday at 5, and don't expect no Madness on the tape deck...I'm not driving an hour through rush hour traffic listening to that!"

John was prevented from any witty comeback by the line being cut almost immediately and he placed his handset back in the hollowed-out part of his desk where it usually resided. "Ungrateful bastard" he thought to himself and the pulled his desk open to check on his latest gadget.

Although there were a few people around in the City with mobile phones John wasn't keen on carrying one. They were huge and ran out of battery very quickly and the thought of being on call 24/7 wasn't particularly attractive to him. He preferred his pager. If someone needed him badly, they could send an alert, which he could ignore if he wanted, and he could also get market updates on it.

With her legendary attention to detail Madelaine had informed him that the pager he currently had would not work in Hong Kong, so he had just received an updated version from his Reuters rep. Unwrapping it he inserted the two small batteries and powered it on. As expected, the green lettering started scrolling across the screen giving regular updates for the market prices that mirrored his current pager. Satisfied, he powered it down again and popped it in the travel pack with the rest of his documents.

"So, you're off to Honkers?" John turned to see Nicola approaching with a sheaf of printouts.

"Yes, got to go and relieve the troops. You been there?"

"We actually lived there for a while when I was very young" replied Nicola. "Daddy worked out there for a while and we came back when I was about five".

"Suppose you had maids and everything?" John probed.

"Well, there did seem to be a few Filipino girls around to do most things, and I loved our Amah".

John wasn't really sure what an Amah was but didn't want to show his ignorance so just nodded.

"Any tips for me then? Local knowledge?"

"Stay away from the Century eggs!" She smiled easily, "they are just disgusting!"

John's knowledge of Century Eggs was on a par with his knowledge of Amahs, so he smiled along with her and resolved to do a bit of asking to find out what they were.

Nicola continued, extracting a couple of sheets from the pile in her arms. "Those World Banks you got hit in this morning are looking really cheap, here's a Rich/Cheap analysis I've done on the Bloomberg. If you can get any more of them, I think I could sell a block to my man at Bank of England".

Having been the beneficiary of her advice before, John was not too proud to accept her recommendation but still wanted to make it look like he knew what he was doing.

"Yeah, I thought they were cheap, so I've been trying to be a good bid in them. Cheers Nic"

"You're welcome, John" she trilled and headed off back to her desk.

As if to show her he was listening he immediately shouted down the box to Grub "Oi Grub, got anything in World Bank 16's?"

"Nothing working mate, there was a seller around first thing, but I think he's all done. You got a care?" came the reply.

I'd be a buyer, but keep it under your hat" John said conspiratorially.

With most brokers John would not profess which way his interest was for fear of them giving their clients the knowledge, but he knew Grub would keep that knowledge to himself to make sure if there were any bonds going in that issue John would get first go at them.

He didn't expect anything that afternoon though. The World Bank issue was the longest maturity issue he traded and therefore one of the most volatile. It directly responded to the movements of the US Government 30-year bond which was generally more active in New York time than the London morning so if you were going to get anything done in it, then it was likely to be in the morning. The afternoon seemed to drag on without much incident and John found himself at a bit of a loose end. His trading book was smaller than usual because of the business trip and the oft quoted phrase "idle hands do the devil's work" could have been written about him. He spent most of the afternoon standing looking around over the horseshoe conveyor belt searching for targets.

This was familiar behaviour on John's part and most of the desk would be unwilling to raise their heads above the ramparts for fear of attracting his wrath. At 4 p.m. however, Jerry Fowler could wait no longer. Jerry was an anomaly in the dealing room, a scouse university graduate with an extremely good degree from Cambridge who refused to modulate his accent at all and steadfastly went back up to Liverpool every other weekend to see his folks. To make things even more incongruous he worked with the Interest Rate Swaps team. Every member of the team (apart from him) seemed to have been pressed from a mould. Cut-glass accents, Hermes ties and Saville Row suits. His mathematical abilities were undeniable though and nothing made people set aside their prejudices more than a nice healthy P and L.

Jerry rose from his desk, shouldered his duffel bag and headed towards the lifts. He thought he'd made it until the familiar rasp of Fieldy floated across the desk. "Youse going bach to Liverpool scouse?" His attempt at a Liverpudlian accent was laughable.

Jerry already knew what was coming. "Dunno how you worked that out Sherlock" he replied, almost to himself.

Fieldy's hand emerged from his pocket brandishing a £20 note above his head. "Here's twenty quid, buy us a couple of houses while you're up there!"

A couple of the traders raised a slight smile at this, but by far the most amused of them all was John himself. It would be at least a couple of weeks before he would use that gag again.

CHAPTER 10

O n his arrival into the office on Monday morning John was very careful to place his suit carrier and case more-or-less out of sight in a seldom visited part of the trading floor. He was very careful to lock both items. The casual observer might have been surprised at the level of mistrust in such an action, but John was not worried about anyone taking anything out of his cases; the risk of incriminatory objects being placed in his luggage was far more likely. One of his brokers, Robbo, was famous for having a collection of dildos in his desk that he would wrap in aluminium foil and put into colleagues' hand luggage so that when it passed through the security scanner the guard would be confronted by a glowing, penis shaped object. Photographs had been cut out from newspapers and stuck over the passport photographs before, and probably the worst case was when a visiting American salesman had stopped in the office for a day, on his way to the AIBD Golf weekend in Cannes. Obviously unaware of the perils of leaving luggage unattended in the office, the traders managed to sneak a fire extinguisher into the flight bag he had his golf clubs in. How he didn't notice the extra weight was baffling, but Taylor Bradford did like to carry a lot of kit.

Satisfied he had taken all reasonable precautions John wandered over to his desk and made himself busy with an almond croissant and cappuccino.

The day dragged and most of John's trading was avoiding taking any new positions on before he left town for the week. He did sit down for a while with Nicola for any further inside knowledge on Hong Kong and discovered that century eggs were actually preserved eggs, that were stored in clay after being pickled and the white would turn translucent blue. He considered Nicola's earlier warning about them superfluous as he couldn't see himself going anywhere near them no matter how many TsingTaos he drunk. Nicola also gave him some useful Cantonese phrases, including "mm goi", which means thank-you. Again, John found this overkill. He told Nicola he rarely used thank-you in English so would probably not bother in Cantonese. At 4.50 p.m. John finally slipped his trench-coat on and headed over to his luggage. A quick survey of the locks assured him that it had not been tampered with and he lifted the suit carrier onto his shoulder and wheeled the case down the corridor to the lifts.

He was a good five yards away from the revolving doors when he heard the thumping of a reggae bass line which told him Delroy was probably already there. Struggling to get the suit carrier through the revolving doors he finally emerged onto the pavement and opened the back door of the cab. He threw the baggage in, jumped in after it and slammed the cab door.

"What the hell is this?" he shouted above the music.

"Barrington Levi mate. Here I come. A classic". Delroy pressed the eject button on the cassette player and looked down to his case to select something a little less contentious for John. Bobby Womack caught his eye and as he pushed it into the slot the intro to "How could you break my heart?" sent the usual shiver down his spine. Eight years old and still sounding so good. He reached up to flick his meter on, checked over his shoulder for oncoming traffic and pulled into the flow of traffic.

"So, where you off to?" Delroy enquired to his passenger.

"Heathrow" was John's single word reply.

"I know that you daft fucker, I mean where are you flying to?"

"Oh Hong Kong." John caught on. "Got a week out there, showing them what it's all about".

Delroy nodded and decided not to prompt any further exchange unless John particularly wanted to chat. Their only common ground would probably be football, and even in the limited discussions they'd had on that it was obvious that John was an advocate of the all-action, kick bollock and bite type of football that Delroy so vehemently opposed. Where was all the artistry and technique in that?

He hoped another notch on the volume would discourage further discussion and the journey passed smoothly with Delroy enjoying the chance to listen to one of his favourite singers. Fittingly, as he pulled up to the terminal entrance Bobby Womack was asking "Where do we go from here?"

John extricated himself from the cab and gave Delroy the £80 indicated on his meter plus another £5 as a tip. "Cheers guv" said Delroy in a Dick Van Dyke cockney accent. He filled in a taxi receipt that John had requested and as he handed it over asked "you want a little something for the journey?" with a cheeky smile on his face.

"Don't be a dick. That's all I need when I get there, three little Chinese blokes giving me an access all areas body search if they suspect something".

"I was just asking!" teased Delroy," If you want me to pick you up when you come back, give me a ring, I'll make sure I've got some on board to get you over the jet lag!"

John just grunted in response and headed into the terminal building. Once through the doors he looked at the screens and ambled over to where a roped-off section for Business and First-Class check-in was reassuringly devoid of a queue.

John decided quickly that he could quite easily get used to travelling like this. From the moment he presented his ticket to the lady on the desk everything became smooth. A dedicated security lane meant he didn't have to wait behind some old people while they took 10 minutes to sort their clothing out, and it also marked him out as a VIP. In particular, he loved the "You can wait in the lounge until all the other passengers have boarded Mr Field and we will call you when the aircraft is ready to leave. "

The BA check-in girl asked him if he knew where the lounge was, and because he wanted to appear like a seasoned traveller, he said he did, grabbed his boarding card and passport and proceeded through security. The BA lounge was thankfully easy to find and on arrival, after dropping his bags by the reception desk, and checking in he presented himself at the bar and viewed the offerings. The man behind the bar welcomed him warmly. "Good evening, Sir. What can I get you?"

After pondering for a second or two John replied, "I'd like something refreshing and cold".

"How about this Chardonnay Sir?" the barman showed him a bottle of Pouilly-Fuisse.

John had drunk some Australian Chardonnay in the past and hated the taste of it. With his best wine-buff look he said to the barman "I'm not keen on Chardonnay to be honest. I'll just have some Champagne".

The barman turned around to replace the rejected Burgundy whilst suppressing a giggle. Most Champagne was at least one third Chardonnay and in fact, for a laugh he may give him a glass of Blanc de Blancs Champagne which was 100% Chardonnay. By the time he had turned around to face his customer, the barman had regained his composure and filled up a flute with the Blanc de Blancs and set a small plate of nuts next to the glass. "There you are Sir".

John took a sip, and said "mm lovely", and picked the plate and glass up to find a comfy armchair to settle down in.

As he was making his mind up where to sit, he noticed another entrant to the lounge, approaching his position at the bar. The newcomer was a very trendy looking blonde lady, slightly taller than John, with shapely legs encased in leather trousers and a fur coat draped over one arm. Her eyes were obscured by a large, and somewhat unnecessary John thought, pair of sunglasses. She looked everything John expected to encounter in this new environment, that he was starting to inhabit. If he could have thought of something to say he would have loved to, but only realised after some moments that he had been regarding her with his mouth open as she approached.

In the end, he didn't have to say anything. As she got closer, she edged her sunglasses partially down her nose so that she could regard him directly and said "Stay just like that. I'll see if I can throw one of these nuts in from here!"

He snapped his mouth shut and tried to think of something smart to reply with but for the moment was temporarily flummoxed.

"How's the Champagne? "She continued.

"Yes lovely, do you want one?" He turned to the barman and in a reflex movement reached into the inside of his jacket to get his wallet before remembering everything was free in here.

The barman, a consummate professional, had already conjured up another flute and was halfway through pouring it out.

"I'm John by the way" he proffered his hand to her as she sipped on her Champagne. It seemed a lifetime until she lowered her glass from her mouth leaving a large smudge of her blood red lipstick on the glass. "Penelope James" she responded, shaking his outstretched hand briefly. "Nice to meet you".

John had fantasised about such things happening as soon as he heard he was taking a business class flight. He was confident there was a good deal of sex going on in the toilets in business class. The stewardesses must all be starved of heterosexual male company with all the male crew being gay. John always saw things in black and white. In his mind he was just opening the door to a whole new chapter in his life.

"Would you like to join me on the sofa over there? "John asked. "You're not meeting anyone are you?"

"Yes, why not?" She picked up her elegant handbag and fur coat and glided over to the sofa John had indicated whilst John followed her, trying to juggle two Champagne glasses and a plate of nuts. This task did not prevent him from admiring the graceful way she walked.

Surprisingly, for someone as devoid of outside interests as John, the conversation flowed freely, and he found himself talking to Penelope more openly than he had talked to many people for a long time. He found out she was a dancer and was on her way back to Tokyo for the last weeks of her contract before returning to England for good. He also found out she was single and hadn't organised a place to live yet when she returned from Japan. By the time a BA uniformed woman was gently tapping on John's shoulder they had emptied the bottle of Blanc de Blancs and seen off a glass of Sake each too. "Mr Field, your flight is now ready for boarding" the gentle but firm voice of the lounge attendant stirred him into action. He looked intently at his reflection in Penelope's sunglasses.

"Can we meet up when you get back?"

"That would be nice," said Penelope, let me take your card.

John remembered the stack of new cards Madeleine had included in his travel pack and carefully presented one to the seated dancer.

Penelope studied it for a while before standing up out of the chair, slipping the card into the ridiculously tight back pocket of her leather trousers and giving John the merest of brushes on the cheek. "Safe flight then"

"You too" replied John and gathered his bags up to walk to the aeroplane.

CHAPTER 11

The flight was somewhat of a let-down for John. His fantasies of young stewardesses, overcome with desire, clad in tight-fitting skirts were soon dispelled by the middle-aged woman who ushered him to his seat and gave him a small leather pouch along with a blanket and small pillow. As he looked around, he failed to see any targets to chat to in the cabin either. Most of the occupants seemed to be older Europeans or Hong Kong residents returning home. He resigned himself to drinking more of the free booze before settling down to the movie. The food was surprisingly good and when the titles on the large TV screen announced "Fatal Attraction" he slipped his headphones on, fully expecting to be asleep by the end of the movie. He wasn't a big filmgoer but as it got under way his interest was sparked. Michael Douglas was a bit of a hero in his eyes, and he couldn't believe it when the nutty bird started kicking off. "What was her problem? Couldn't she just accept it was a bit of fun over the weekend?" In fact, by the end of it, John found that a movie he had quite enjoyed watching to start off with had become a little unsettling. John asked himself what he could learn from this and thought back to a line from his favourite TV comedy, "Only Fools and Horses". "Your idea of safe sex Delboy is not giving a bird your telephone number!". Yes, if Michael Douglas had been more careful, he could have got away with it. The notion of not committing the indiscretion in the first place was a consideration that didn't even cross John's mind.

He dropped off into a deep sleep after the film finished and did not stir until he was aware of the lights coming on again and an announcement that there would be a service of light snacks and beverages before the landing into Hong Kong, some 90 minutes away. The long flight meant the second shift of cabin crew were working now and as they wandered around dispensing snacks John wondered where the other team were sleeping. His mouth felt very dry, and he greedily downed the glass of water the new young attendant offered him. He made fast work of the snacks and then ordered some strong coffee. When he landed it would be late afternoon in Hong Kong and he was expected to drop his bags at the hotel and then go straight to meet Roger Forsyth downtown.

Besides Nicola's advice on Century eggs, she had also warned John about the landing experience into Kai Tak airport in Hong Kong. He assumed she was just being a "bit of a girl" and was sure passenger aircraft of this size couldn't throw themselves about much, but nevertheless, with a window seat he was full of anticipation as he heard the captain say, "Cabin crew, seats for landing". The degree of banking the plane went into was certainly a little alarming, but even more surprising was the proximity of residential buildings to the wing tips. On the flat roof of one of these buildings was painted a huge "turn left" white arrow and he could make out the features of a small Chinese woman hanging out washing seemingly unaware of the huge jet above her head. Her two children were aware however and gleefully waved at the aircraft's occupants as it grazed the rooftops of the bustling city. John fully expected to get off the plane to see lines of washing draped around the wings they were so close.

His fears were ungrounded though and as he heard the P.A. announce, "welcome to Hong Kong where the local time is four fifteen in the afternoon" he started to think about the coming week and tonight's "handover meeting".

Roger Forsyth was one of the two European traders working for Regal Bank in Hong Kong. He was a notorious practical joker and John was already practicing being on his guard for any of his little schemes. He suspected the most likely would be some form of booby trap on the desk in the morning...shoe polish on the earpiece or a prawn left in his drawer to decompose. Yes, there would have to be a full sit-rep carried out before sitting down tomorrow morning. Roger was flying out first thing, so that would be typical of him. John thought he was a bit of a knob but like the other traders in London, they had to tolerate him. Together with Faisal, the other Hong Kong trader, they held the fates of the London traders in their hands overnight, and if you didn't look after them you were likely to find a nasty surprise on your book when you came in in the morning.

John was pleased to receive a nice official stamp in his passport, further credentials of his jet-set existence, but was more than a little disappointed not to have a limousine to his hotel. Madelaine had told him regular taxis were easier and it wasn't a long trip anyway. There were plenty of the distinctive red taxis lined up outside and he didn't have to wait long to reach the head of the queue. As his cab pulled up the driver seemed to have opened his door and scurried around to the pavement almost before the vehicle had stopped moving. The diminutive man picked John's bags up, deposited them in the already opened boot of the car and virtually shouted "Where to Sir?"

After his week was over in Hong Kong, John would come to realise that the driver was not actually shouting at him but that this was regular volume for Hong Kong. You could tell when they were speaking Cantonese because that was even louder. For now, John just guessed the guy might be a bit deaf so shouted back "Mandarin Oriental" and got in the back seat of the car.

The dark opulence of the reception area of the hotel was mightily impressive and as he filled in his registration details at the front desk John wondered what his room would be like. It was after 5 p.m. by the time the bell boy had deposited his luggage in the room and as he was due to meet Roger close by for dinner at 6.00 p.m., he decided a quick shower was in order. He swiftly hung up his other suit and threw some shirts and underwear in a drawer before grappling with the unfamiliar controls of the hotel's all-singing, all-dancing, shower head for a somewhat unfulfilling experience.

He was back down at reception by 5.45 p.m. and after enquiring about the location of their dinner from reception he marched confidently out into the evening haze.

He reached Jimmy's Kitchen, a long-established Hong Kong eatery in less than five minutes and was there before Roger Forsyth so ordered a beer and started perusing the menu at the bar to check if Roger had set him up with a place where he had to cram a lot of "foreign muck" down his neck. The menu was reassuringly European and to be honest almost all British. He'd just put the menu down when a hearty slap on his shoulder announced Roger's arrival.

"Welcome to Hong Kong Sassenach, how was your flight?" Roger's soft Edinburgh burr sounded more pronounced than it did over the phone and John stood up to welcome him replying "Alright sweaty sock...yep flight was all good. How are you mate?"

"Yep fantastic...looking forward to my week off."

Roger gestured to the barman who placed a Tsing Tao down on the bar in front of them without exchanging a word and the two colleagues clinked bottles and greedily attacked their beers.

As the meal progressed Roger filled John in on events in the office and everyday life in Hong Kong and told him the office location. John laughed when he remembered Madelaine asking him in London if he needed directions from the hotel to the office. Roger told him you could see Jardine House by looking out of the window of his hotel! It was also distinguishable by the fact it was one of the few skyscrapers in Hong Kong to have round, port-hole shaped windows. Supposedly it was for this reason the building was nick-named by locals "the building of a thousand arseholes". The fact that the building housed a large number of European bankers, could have been an alternative theory.

It wasn't long before John was waving his Amex card at the waiter to settle their bill and Roger informed him they were off for the second part of their evening. They hailed a cab directly outside Jimmy's and Roger directed him tersely to "Crazy 88 bar Wanchai ".

John had heard a lot about Wanchai and was looking forward to it immensely. Their entrance to the bar did not disappoint him as they were immediately latched on to by two attractive Philippine girls clad in skimpy tops and cut-off denim hot pants.

On reflection, John could not really remember much of their conversation. The girls' halting English, and the thumping music meant most things had to be repeated once or twice and after about an hour in which the girl at John's side had got quite tactile, he saw Roger slide off the bar stool he was perched on and said to John "mate I'm off to bed, my flight's at stupid o'clock in the morning. Why don't you stay for a while...she looks keen! I'll clear the tab on the way out".

"Ok Roger, I'll just finish this up and go myself...have a good holiday" John saw no need to leave right away and was enjoying Maria (as she had told him she was called) tickling his inner thigh lightly with her fingers which occasionally strayed to the growing bulge in his trousers. With Roger out of the way the other girl, devoid of any unattended targets in the bar, decided to double-team with Maria and pointing at John's crotch whispered in his ear "we should go somewhere quieter".

Putting up the merest of resistance John found himself dragged into a room at the back of the bar bedecked with draped curtains and large cushions strewn around the floor. The girls directed him to a comfy looking sofa at the back of the room and then slid to the floor and directed their attention to his trouser zip. For some reason, it was at this point that he looked at his watch, which was still on London time and realised New York would be opening now and he had a bit of a short position on.

Whilst not wanting to disturb the work going on below his waistline, he slipped his hand into his jacket pocket and eased out his pager. After a couple of FTSE and Dow Jones numbers scrolled by, he was satisfied to see the U.S. Long bond was moving significantly lower on the opening. His glance caught the two heads working away at him just behind the pager. "You're a God Fieldy!" he thought to himself, pocketed the pager, laid back and closed his eyes.

CHAPTER 12

With his passenger out of the back of the cab Delroy mooted whether to join the rank of taxis waiting for passengers at Heathrow or just drive himself home. The traffic would be crap either way and he might as well get a return journey out of it. As he pulled up behind a row of perhaps 20 black cabs in front of him, he ejected the Bobby Womack tape from his machine and considered the next choice up. Delroy's musical tastes were wide and eclectic, and his flirtation with piano lessons for a couple of years had given him access to, and an appreciation of classical music, uncommon for most of his contemporaries. As he prepared for the next fare, he slipped in Debussy's "L'apres-midi d'un faun" and pumped up the volume to let the shimmering sounds flood all over him. He'd have to turn it off when a punter got in, but until then he was in a better place. Reggae wasn't the only thing you needed some hefty speakers for; classical music could have such a contrast in dynamics that you needed it pumped up so that you could hear the quiet bits. He'd only got halfway through the 10-minute prelude before reaching the front of the queue where an orthodox Jewish couple with two small children were waiting with their cases and requested an address in Stamford Hill. Delroy thought to himself he could have guessed where they were going before they even asked. Most Hassidic Jews wore wide brimmed hats which spawned the nickname "Stamford Hill cowboys", or "frummers" as many old east-enders would call them using the Yiddish derived word for pious. The only surprise to Delroy was that they were getting a cab. Surely a Volvo estate parked at the airport would have been customary?

As the family boarded the cab, he had time to give himself a mental dressing down. "Why are you making assumptions about them? If someone looked at me and made assumptions because of what I looked like, wouldn't I be pissed off?"

As usual with his mental debates, he decided this needed further examination.

His train of thought continued.

It would be better if people just took one another as they found them rather than making assumptions based upon pre-conceived prejudices but when all was said and done, you can't affect what goes on in someone's head. For society to function you've got to make sure people control their actions; actions are visible and have repercussions... you can't tell people what to think can you? Or can you? Isn't that why we educate them?

The voice from behind him interrupted his reverie and prompted him to pull away from the rank and mentally plot a course to Stamford Hill. When that was decided upon, his thoughts turned to food. He hadn't eaten since breakfast and was feeling very peckish. Dropping off at Stamford Hill would mean it would be easy to stop at a jerk chicken place in Ridley Road, a perennial favourite of his, and there was also a good fish and chip shop there. Glancing in his rear mirror he wondered how many of the guys round his flats knew that fish and chips was a Jewish import. Now it was "The Great British takeaway" and the BNP members would eschew other foods as being "foreign shit". We probably need to wait another 50 years or so before jerk chicken and ackee and saltfish are added to the list of British staples!

His journey to Stamford Hill was without incident and with his orange light off, he felt himself inexorably drawn to the West Indian food shop in Dalston. With some curry goat on top of a pile of rice and beans, Gregory Isaac's Night Nurse album on the cassette player, Delroy was feeling extremely mellow and was totally unprepared for his car phone disturbing him.

He was quite a meticulous man and took care to fully wipe his hands and mouth before finally pressing the handset against his ear and answering. "DJ here".

"Delboy, it's Andy" came a rough voice from phone. "I need a favour mate. Can I use your garage for a week or so?"

"Suppose so" was the reply, through a mouthful of goat. "Don't like leaving my cab outside to be honest though. When do you need it?"

Andy's next words were a little more contrite. "Well, I've actually put some stuff in there already. You'd have trouble getting your moped in there let alone the cab! Listen mate, it won't be for long. Some little fucker has grassed on me, and I got a tip that the old bill were gonna raid my joint and I've just had a load of Charlie delivered so I had to move it out sharpish".

Being a person to avoid ever seeming flustered Delroy tried to come to terms with the statement but still sounded incredulous when he replied. "So right now, my garage is stuffed full of cocaine?"

"Mostly yea, and there's some expensive kettles in there too! Perhaps you should have a look; see if you fancy one of them. All kosher Rolexes!" Andy replied.

"I aint going anywhere near that garage 'til you've moved it all out" warned Delroy, "and for fuck's sake do it a bit lively".

"Cheers mate. One week, top whack. I promise. Just got to get hold of the little rat who put me in the frame. I know who he is" Andy rang off and Delroy sat still for a while turning over the knowledge in his mind. This was a potential outcome that he had thought about before. It's hard to be half in and half out with criminals. Once you're involved, you're involved, and the depth of that involvement was not under your control. He resumed munching at the goat and resolved that no degree of thinking was going to help him on this one. The only way through this was to completely forget about it for a week and hope Andy was as good as his word.

When he had finally sucked all the goat bones clean, he deliberately packed up the polystyrene container and the empty Lilt can and put them in the dustbin outside the shop.

Before pulling away he decided he needed a new soundtrack. The ambiance created by Gregory Isaacs and some curry goat had completely disappeared. He fished in his case and came out with a cassette entitled "random" and stuck it in the slot.

Curtis Mayfield was singing "Freddie's Dead" and the familiar lyrics seemed to be doubly meaningful.

Everybody's misused him
Ripped him up and abused him
Another junkie plan
Pushing dope for the man
A terrible blow
But that's how it goes
A Freddie's on the corner now
If you want to be a junkie, wow
Remember Freddie's dead.

Delroy was convinced there wasn't some greater power overseeing the world, but he was also sure that if there was, this would be the sort of thing to expect. Veiled warnings, expressed in strange portents, like burning bushes. As usual his mental weighing of the problem came down more on the side of realism rather than fantasy and ended up with him telling himself "Don't be such a wanker ... it's just a coincidence".

As he reached his garage and pulled onto the concrete apron in front of it, he stared acutely at the metal door, keenly looking for signs that something had changed and that it was obvious there was a King's ransom in stolen watches and cocaine stashed behind the ordinary looking cream door, but it looked much the same as always. Before locking the cab up, Delroy disengaged the front section of his cassette player, an anti-theft precaution which he would normally forego when he was inside the garage and rescued his precious tapes from the cab. Things would be really bad if he got caught with a garage full of drugs AND his music got nicked. When he reached his flat, he must have taken a peek from his sister's old bedroom, which had a view of the garage, about five times before finally going to bed.

CHAPTER 13

The familiar fog of a hangover wreathed John Field's eyes as he rolled over to turn off the automatic wakeup call he had ordered on check-in and within a few minutes he had pieced together where he actually was. Probing further into his memories he allowed himself a smirk at the thought of two women giving him oral sex whilst he made money on trading. The thought seemed to perk him up and further reinforce in his mind that he was not just any ordinary individual but a special one, and special ones did not suffer from hangovers. He swiftly rolled out of bed and forced himself into a cold shower which he soon wimped out of and turned the hot tap up. Exiting the shower with a towel around his waist he was just in time to open the door for the in-room breakfast service he had wisely ordered the day before. The intake of food and plenty of coffee went a long way towards rectifying his hangover and by the time he was stepping out of the hotel for the short walk to Jardine House he was feeling at least 70% normal. After finally getting through security to get into his office and being given a temporary pass for the turnstiles downstairs he finally arrived at Roger's vacant desk.

He walked up behind Faisal, who stood up, turned to greet him and shook him warmly by the hand. "Welcome to paradise mate!". John returned the handshake and smiled at Faisal who he'd met once before when he visited the London offices. "Is this my seat?" He gestured at the chair next to Faisal which had more screens in front of it than most of the others in the room.

"Yep, that's Roger's chair...yours for the week" confirmed Faisal.

John regarded the well-worn chair much like a pathologist starting a postmortem. He felt the chair to see if it had been soaked the night before...another common practical joke. Then, searching for a tissue he picked up the handset to check it for shoe polish. When that proved negative, he gingerly pulled each drawer of the unit under the desk open to assure himself there were no nasty surprises there either. His performance was attracting some curious glances from the local staff on the trading floor, but he didn't care. He was sure there was something to be found. After a while the Hong Kong people in the office concluded it must be just another weird Gweilo thing. Gweilo was a Cantonese nickname for Europeans. They soon lost interest and got back to their calls.

John decided that if Roger had left anything to catch him, he could not spend any more time looking for it and cautiously slipped his jacket off and sat down in the chair as Faisal explained how the screens were set up and how he could get up the services he wanted.

"Before you get started, let's walk you around and introduce you" said Faisal and got out of his chair.

On his circumnavigation of the trading floor John discovered most of the local hires had given themselves European first names followed by their Chinese family name. This produced some amusing combinations. John's favourites were Mary Li and Ivan Ho. It was Ivan who proved the most sociable, asking John how his flight was and if he went out last night.

"Yes, I met Roger for dinner and then we went to Crazy 88 bar for a few drinks" John told him.

"Hahaha" Ivan's laugh was like a machine gun. "Very famous bar that is! You like?"

"Oh yes, top place. Do you go there?" John replied.

"No no, only Gweilos go there who like ladies with dick! Everyone there is a ladyboy...that's why so famous!"

Fieldy's face was anything but inscrutable as he ran through the night's activities with this new information to hand. Luckily Ivan was the last visit on his tour around the room and he had time to go back to his desk and compose himself. He decided he did not need to look for any prawns hidden anywhere. Roger had stitched him up like a kipper and he was mad as hell. His mood was not helped by looking at the screens in front of him. The movement down in the long bond on the US open last night had completely reversed and now rather than sitting on a nice profit he was offside twice as much.

Suddenly the hangover seemed to be reasserting itself. "Where's the coffee machine? "he shouted at Faisal, ignoring the fact he was on the phone.

Faisal gestured with his free hand to the back of the room and John followed his pointed direction to find a small kitchen and a couple of doors with the male and female symbols on denoting toilets.

A sudden impulse took him, and he went into the toilet and undid his flies to examine his now "violated" penis. After some rationalisation he concluded examining it would change nothing and he sat down on the toilet pan to think a while longer. As his eyes drifted higher toward the top of the door he saw several handprints at roughly head level. Something else Nicola had told him sprang to mind. A lot of the lower-level hires in Hong Kong had come from quite a rural or under privileged background. They were accustomed to using a hole in the ground as a lavatory, so when it came to toilets such as he was sitting on, they would stand on the pan with their hands against the door.

"Fuck, that probably means I'm sitting in someone's footprints" he thought.

Bouncing back upright he flushed the toilet, washed his hands vigorously and determined that he would try to save all future toilet visits for the hotel.

By the time he returned to his desk he had his game face on and began prodding at the keypads in front of him to get the required screens he wanted to look at and to calculate how much he should change prices in view of the U.S. market's overnight moves. The exercise gave him a welcome distraction from thinking about the preceding night's activities. A couple of hours passed relatively quickly and with very little disturbance from the salesforce. The background noise was generally at a much lower level than that in London apart from the occasional phone pick-up by Hong Kong salespeople which always seemed to be done at a volume that negated the need for amplification at all. "Wei!" seemed to be shouted down a handset at regular intervals followed by a conversation at more normal levels. As they reached mid-morning, he turned to face Faisal. "It always this quiet? I ain't been asked a single price".

"It can be" Faisal replied. "Business here tends to be a bit less often but bigger size when it comes along. I sometimes think they are waiting to catch you. We talk to a fair few Central Banks and when they come in it can be huge. Also, I'm not always sure we're the only ones seeing it. Makes things difficult if you're being asked to bid a lump while someone else is already out there hammering the bid" Fieldy made a mental note. He considered he'd already been turned over last night. It wasn't going to happen again. He also decided that he was falling out of love with business trips after a day of his first one. He loved all the fuss over him of executive lounges, business class seats and fancy hotels, but actually working in Hong Kong, which was the meat in the sandwich, was quickly losing its allure. Worse still, the locals wanted to take him out tonight. "What sort of god-awful food am I going to have to suffer this evening?" A momentary vision of a feast scene from "Indiana Jones and the Temple of Doom" sprang into his mind. For a moment he found the images quite disconcerting, but then, as his eyes slid around the imaginary table he saw Indie's companion, Kate Capshaw, or at least it should have been Kate Capshaw. In John's vision she had the face of Penelope James, the chance encounter he had in the lounge at Heathrow. Suddenly all thoughts of Century eggs and deep-fried beetles disappeared, and he was reminded that he definitely wanted to try to catch up with her again. With his thoughts turning to a much more positive horizon he began to feel a little more optimistic.

"Mr John, Mr John!" Ivan was on his feet on the other side of the room. "Please bid 15 million EIB 3 years for a very good account!"

With a sigh, Penelope was tucked away into a temporary file in the back of John's head, and he set about tracing his finger down his blotter to the issue in question and checking out where the U.S. three year was.

"Yeah, yeah" replied John, "they're all good accounts ".

"99.35 on the line Ivan....as long as he's not shopping it all round town." John was pleased to finally have something to concentrate on and hoped there would be more... it would at least help to pass the week quickly.

CHAPTER 14

At Plummer's, despite the absence of Fieldy , Grub was looking forward to an interesting week. On Tuesday there was going to be a Big Mac eating challenge and then on Thursday there would be settlement of a huge unofficial market-making exercise based upon the number of 2p pieces Patrick O'Hanlon could get in his foreskin.

The Big Macs were due to be consumed by one of the youngest members of the broking team who had recently joined from school aged 16 because he was related to Kevin, Grub's boss. He was mostly tasked with carrying papers around and got nowhere near any calls. A couple of weeks ago he foolishly commented whilst eating a Big Mac, "I could eat another five of them".

"Like fuck you could" was the reply from a gnarled old broker sitting next to him at the time.

On their return to the office the challenge was discussed, and rules formulated. Young Barry would have to consume six Big Macs between 12.00 and 1.30p.m. and he was allowed to drink some water with it. Despite agreeing to the challenge Barry had realised after some time there was very little upside for him. If he was successful, he would have a very full belly that he hadn't paid for, if unsuccessful he would still have a full belly and his wallet would be lighter to the tune of 6 Big Macs!

Nevertheless, he was sure he could do it and if you were hoping to progress in the bear pit that was the broking world you had to show a bit of bravado now and then.

Whilst Barry stood to profit very little from the exercise, his colleagues had taken to making a market on how many he would finish in the allotted time. There was much more to win or lose on this and as Tuesday neared, the market had settled down at 3.75/4.25. Barry considered buying at 4.25 because he was so sure he could do it, but that also meant that if he didn't complete the challenge not only would he lose money, but he would also have to pay for the burgers. He decided not to participate in the betting for now and when he arrived in the office on Tuesday morning, he was questioned by the brokers who were long of the market and wanted him to succeed. Never had so much interest been taken in him and his previous night's eating regime.

Things were so tense that he was even prevented from ordering anything in the morning breakfast run for fear of it affecting his capacity later on.

As the clocks ticked over to 12.01, and the clients' lights stopped flashing, Barry pulled himself upright and started munching into the first of his burgers that had been delivered just five minutes before. Barry had always had a prodigious appetite but his age, and metabolism, meant that he maintained a very slim figure which belied his capacity. The first two burgers disappeared very quickly, and in his peripheral hearing he was aware of some trading going on around the 4.5/5 level as two brokers behind him made a trade.

With a small sip of water, Barry began on the third and Grub, looking on from behind, grew more confident he was right to be long. He was sure Barry would polish them all off and perhaps he would use his winnings to short some more on the Patrick O 'Hanlon foreskin market. There was no way he was getting more than twenty 2p pieces in his foreskin, no way.

By ten past one, Barry was on his last burger, the market was effectively closed and only the most desperate were not paying up on their debts, waiting vainly to see if he left any. Grub was doubly pleased. He'd won some money and still had time to nip out for a couple of pints.

"Oi Barry!" he shouted at the gangling youngster. "Come over the road with me to the Ten Bells. I'll buy you something to wash that lot down with!"

As Kevin Conolly watched the unlikely pair walk out of the trading room, he hoped Barry would perhaps not fill in his mum on all the details of his day. Barry was the son of Kevin's older sister, and whilst she was reasonably streetwise, her hopes of a lucrative career in finance for her 16-year-old son probably did not include a burger eating contest followed by speed drinking three or four pints in the nearest strip joint in Shoreditch. Kevin resolved to have a whisper in his ear when he got back, (provided Grub left him in any state to understand instructions).

Grub was obviously aware of Barry's family connection so after 3 pints, and a slightly green pallor clouding the youngster's face, it was decided to return to the office.

On his return, Grub's next concern was Thursday. Apparently, the whole Patrick O'Hanlon bet had started after a football match that Plummer's played against a traders' team at QPR's ground, Loftus Road. The game had been traumatic from the start for Grub, who had been a half decent footballer at school. The kits that were supplied had not been designed for people of such stature and despite finally finding a pair of shorts he could slither into like a second skin there was not a lot of room for movement. QPR were one of the few professional clubs to have had an astro- turf pitch installed and to say it was tricky was an understatement. Grub had actually played on one of the first ones in England at Hackney Marshes for his district side. The ball bounced as if it were solid rubber and any slip or slide tackle resulted in carpet type burns that would mean your trousers stuck to the graze for the next three days.

Being aware of the change in his physique since his school days, Grub played his first few passes very simply. His touch had always been good and if you can move the ball on after one or two touches at football it makes the game very easy. After 10 or 15 minutes he had realised that half the market team were pretty useless and decided it was time for a bit of showboating. Unfortunately for Grub, the ball can hold up on astroturf, and as he tried to execute a perfect Maradona turn between two of the opposition players the ball got stuck under his feet and he tripped himself up, falling to the floor in the most unwieldy of moves and splitting his shorts at the same time.

The whip-crack noise of his shorts being torn was greeted with an hilarious reaction from his team- mates and although his only physical damage was a graze to his knee, he decided now was a good time to limp off and feign injury.

It was for this reason that he wasn't in the showers when the subject of Patrick O'Hanlon's foreskin was brought up.

Having won the game easily, the banter in the brokers' showers was very good natured. There was the normal carry-on of one of the players continually adding shampoo to another's head so that he could seemingly never get all the bubbles out and then Patrick made his appearance. "Jesus mate, did you get given the wrong sized knob with that skin?" One of the brokers did not believe in standing on ceremony.

Patrick gazed down, as if expecting to see something different from what he normally saw there, and then when realising that it was the same as ever, he raised his head again to respond to the jibe. "If you want a big one, you've got to have some growing room! You wouldn't believe how many 2p pieces I can get in there".

"Don't tell me" was the reply. "Let's make a market".

That was how it started. Patrick was forbidden from letting anyone know exactly how many he could get in there and forbidden from taking a position. After a few days the market settled to around the 20 mark.

In-depth analysis of the market would reveal that anyone who was in the showers at the time was invariably a buyer. Seeing is believing. By the time Grub heard about the bet he was safely ensconced in the club bar from where he had watched the remainder of the game. "Twenty 2p pieces? Yours mate, all day long"

He didn't have any copper coins on him so got the only change he had out of his pockets and stacked the three, pound coins in front of him on the bar and visualised. They were much thicker than 2p pieces obviously but still...20?

His next piece of research was a trip to the gents, where he offered up the 3 coins he had in his jacket against his own foreskin. His mind was decided. After putting the coins back in his pocket, presumably for some unsuspecting bartender to handle later, he zipped up his flies and walked back into the bar to trade some more. Twenty was definitely too high.

Unlike the burger challenge on Tuesday, the 2p challenge needed very few rules or time constraints. As on Tuesday the count was set for 12.00 p.m. and at 11.55 a.m. there was already a gaggle of expectant brokers gathered around Patrick's desk. All the guys who were short of the market had requested that one of the females from the office should officiate, hoping that any tumescence she induced in Patrick's member would reduce space. Not unsurprisingly, female volunteers for this task were in short supply so at 12.00p.m. Veg (Terry Wilson) turned up at Patrick's desk with a bag of 2p pieces and a pair of bright yellow Marigold gloves on in case he had to handle the currency afterwards. This was a signal for Patrick, very unashamedly to stand up, drop his pants and trousers and engage upon a series of what might be called "Warm-up exercises"; dragging the skin at the end of his penis to unimaginable lengths. Gasps of amazement started to be heard from brokers gathered around who hadn't been in the showers with him. Suddenly the 20/21 market faded and offers were very hard to find. As he started carefully placing the coins, Grub realised he had just got this one wrong and would lose far more than he'd made on Big Macs on Tuesday. As Patrick's count moved past 20 some of the guys who were short started trying to introduce rules such as ""You can't hold it with your hands" in an attempt to limit the damage , but these protests were waved away and when there was not a millimetre of space left the coins were allowed to cascade back to the desk like the weirdest of fruit machines where Veg, resplendent in his yellow gloves scooped them up like a slip fielder and verified the amount.

"Twenty-eight, twenty-eight" he boomed across the room like a town crier. The throng around Patrick quickly dispersed and bets were settled along with quiet mumblings about what they'd just seen.

Grub was still stunned and sitting at his desk he wondered whether he ought to call Ross and Norris McWhirter about this. How funny would it be to see Patrick and his unfeasibly large foreskin in the Guinness book of records, or showing his talents on the Blue Peter Show?

He'd made £200 pound on the Big Macs but lost more than twice that on Patrick and concluded that eating was something he knew about, and foreskins weren't. You deserve to lose money betting on things you know nothing about. On the bright side it was Thursday. Punishment night. He was due to take a Japanese customer to a Teppanyaki place, Aiyoku Kaku, up by the Mansion House tonight. He'd been there a few times before and really enjoyed it. The highly skilled Japanese chef there had taken a liking to him and was now in the habit of providing a bit of theatre on each visit by flicking pieces of food from the grill straight into Grub's mouth. As some of his colleagues had commented "you don't have to be highly skilled to hit a target like that!" If all went well, he could get the customer pissed by about 8.30 p.m. and then slide off to meet Robbo at Blues. He said his bird had her mate in town this week and she was a screamer. Happy days!

CHAPTER 15

The three inches of snow on top of Delroy's cab just gave him another excuse to curse Andy O'Brien under his breath. Normally his taxi would have been cosily nestled in the garage overnight but because of the unexpected shipment last week it was outside, exposed to the worst March snowstorm he could remember. He had a brush and scraper in the garage but was steadfastly against going in there until the offending articles were relocated. He knew it was stupid really. If it was discovered, there was only one person liable for the blame and there was no real long-term future in telling the Old Bill (or Babylon as his black mates called them) that it belonged to Andy. Still, he felt some sort of detachment by not looking at it and could almost persuade himself that it may have been moved already.

His leather gloves helped him get most of the snow from the cab and he fished out an old plastic membership card from a nightclub to help scrape the ice off the screen. Although the cab was running it was taking a mighty long time to warm up and when he finally thought the cab was sufficiently drivable, he gratefully got into the driving seat. He clapped his gloves together to get rid of the last vestiges of snow and surveyed the wintry scene in front of him through the windscreen.

There were only a few tyre tracks in the virgin snow. Delroy had made an effort to get up early that day as he'd received a call last Friday from John asking if he could pick him up from Heathrow. When Delroy heard the time of the landing he had flatly refused, but after some cajoling, and promises from John to purchase a "good few bags of Colombian Marching Powder" he reluctantly agreed. Sitting there, staring at the weather, he wondered whether flights could be cancelled. Pandemonium normally breaks out in England when the weather strays anywhere outside a ten-degree range thought Delroy to himself. "Rah, if we were in charge of Canada's airports, I bet you couldn't fly there for half the year!"

Despite these fears, he edged the cab gently into the snow, trying not to turn the steering wheel too acutely for fear of the wheels spinning on the slushy mix. He needn't have worried too much. He found after some time that the two jackets he was wearing meant gentle rotations were physically all he could manage anyway and by the time he got onto Hackney Road, where the gritters had been busy, he was able to resume something like normal driving.

The fact he was on his way to pick up John reminded him that it was a full week since he had received the surprise phone call from Andy. He resolved to call his old friend tonight and try to insist that he'd looked after it long enough. The illicit goods in his garage had provided him with a restless week. Even his usual escape from all earthly worries, 90 minutes of football, had been denied him because of the carpet of snow on the pitches. He'd even tried to nick a game with a mate's Sunday League side but that was cancelled too. It was probably a blessing in disguise. Sunday League football in East London could be very dangerous to play, particularly for players of Delroy's skill level. Shaven headed thugs, still half-drunk from Saturday night's activities, hacking at anyone who had the temerity to exhibit any "fancy-Dan" techniques on the pitch. Delroy could look after himself, but did he really need it?

He loved his music, he loved his football, and both could give him a clarity of mind and a tranquillity that he found difficult to attain by any other means. One of his mates had commented that they felt the same way about sex. Delroy had quickly replied "yes, but football last 90 minutes!". His football this season had been going particularly well. His manager at the Isthmian League side he played for was a great advocate the game being played more like the Brazilians played it, and training sessions were innovatively enjoyable. Drills could sometimes involve keeping the ball off the ground for long periods of time and full-backs, traditional solid defenders in the time-honoured English fashion, were often found as far up the pitch as their attacking colleagues. He also made players try to learn new techniques, like using the outside of their foot a la Brazilians. Delroy's manager indulged him and forgave the occasional faux pas because the inspirational passes he could produce were worth the wait. As such Delroy didn't look upon it as a job, but he did get paid a tidy sum. Luckily this was all paid in cash, so as far as the Inland Revenue were aware, his declared income left him with a very slim tax bill at the end of the year. With the money coming in from his distribution in the City, his regular taxi fares, and his football, he could see a future that perhaps would allow him to build up enough reserves to cut contact with the likes of Andy, but he knew it wouldn't be easy.

"Speak of the Devil and he will appear" was one of his mum's old sayings and sure enough, the minute Andy swam into mind, Delroy's mobile chirped at him.

"DJ here." His normal response.

"Where are you? In a jazz club?" Andy enquired.

Delroy ejected the Errol Garner cassette he was listening to, and presumed Andy was being facetious. Even late-night jazz clubs would be doing well to still be banging out tunes at 7.a.m, and as Andy had called him on the mobile, he'd know full well where he was.

"Listen mate, there'll be a Brophy's removals truck at your garage in around an hour. He'll back right up, and with the doors flapped open nobody will see a thing. In any case, with all this snow around a bit more white stuff isn't going to be noticed!" Andy sounded quite cheerful on the other end of the phone.

"Not before time Andy. Don't mind telling you I'll sleep a bit easier with that lot out of my lock-up"!

He did his best to not sound grateful. He wanted to convey to Andy that he was enormously discomfited by the surprise arrival.

"To be honest I don't know what you're so pissed off about. You have regular deliveries from me in there all the time...do you think the quantity is going to make that much difference if you got raided?" Andy had picked up on his mood.

"Well, I'm sure the sentence would be different for someone knocking out a few bags here and there to me being looked upon as Bethnal Green's answer to Pablo Escobar!" Delroy countered.

"Mate, they'd throw the book at you, they'd know it was mine and threaten you with plenty of bird unless you grassed on me. Which I know you wouldn't. Anyhow, it will all be my problem again in a couple of hours and your precious cab can get its home back. Drive safely!" Andy hung up without waiting for a reply and as he put the phone down and looked up, Delroy saw the exit for Heathrow approaching. As he stuck his left-hand indicator and slowed behind the file of traffic pulling off the M25, even slower than usual with the inclement weather, he thought over Andy's words. He was right of course. It's like being pregnant. You either are or you're not. He had been storing cocaine in his garage for some time now. For the last week it had just been a hell of a lot more. He knew the logic was inescapable, but he also knew he would sleep more soundly with the goods somewhere else.

He reached down and re-inserted the cassette he had been listening to. Garner's Concert by the Sea was a classic and as he listened to "It's alright with me" Delroy wondered, as he often did, how a man who could not read music could produce such artistry. His left hand sounded as if someone else was playing it, whilst his right hand flew about behind the rhythmic background on a totally different schedule. The garage, the cocaine, the weather all faded to nothingness as Delroy lapped up the familiar riffs. He wondered what it would have been like to be sitting listening to the concert in Carmel. He'd have to make the most of it...he couldn't see Fieldy buying into Errol Garner when he got him in the cab...not at this volume anyway!

CHAPTER 16

As Delroy's cab neared Heathrow to meet the Hong Kong flight another long-haul Jumbo had already disgorged its passengers into the arrivals hall and the occupants of ANA flight number 101 from Tokyo were patiently queueing at passport control. John would have been surprised to see Penelope James in the main body of the throng, conspicuous by her stiletto heeled height advantage over the majority of bland looking Japanese salary men dressed in remarkably similar suits. She had a friend in the BA lounge at Heathrow and hadn't seen the need to tell John that she got let into the lounge whenever she travelled but still flew economy. Despite her opulent appearance, Penelope James liked to watch the pennies. ANA were the cheapest carrier by far to Tokyo, and as her job involved a lot of time spent with the type of customers that she was sharing the queue with. It was no great hardship suffering the slightly tighter seat sizes.

As the queue edged forwards, she eased her passport open and studied the picture. Vanity had made her take at least five different versions before settling on the one embossed onto the page and she now wistfully studied the seven-year-old image staring back at her, with its enigmatic look and unlined face. She felt the last few years had taken a toll, and not only physically. Tokyo was a claustrophobic city, accommodation expensive and small, and the only friends to discuss things with were generally other "dancers" at the club. Another glance down at her passport took her to the "Date of Birth "field. Another reminder of the biological clock that she seemed to feel ticking more noisily lately. Her eyes finally alighted on another field. "Name" Rita Jarvis.

She had started using "Penelope James" some years ago and thought about having a more upmarket name long before that. Her justification for using "Penelope James" when she reached Tokyo was, ostensibly that the majority of Japanese speakers can't pronounce the letter R easily. When she was told that in Japanese there is little distinction between an R and an L she had to think again. So Penny it was in the club. Or Penny-San to the Japanese businessmen. The real cachet that she thought was associated with her new upmarket name would be lost on anyone non-British anyway in her opinion.

Once through passport control, she made her way to the baggage carousel and waited to see the shiny pink case she had picked up six months ago in a department store in Ginza shuffle up the conveyor belt. Had this been a European flight she may have acted a little forlornly waiting for some eager man to help her off with the case.

Scanning around she decided she could probably bench press fifty percent more than most of the people waiting around and smartly hefted the case onto the shiny marble floor, pulled out the extendable handle and made her way to the exit.

Her steps were purposeful, the long flight had given her time to consider. When she told John her contract was up in Tokyo it was slightly inaccurate. She had decided to end this stage in her life. Her dancing days, which in truth involved little dancing and more being pawed at by drunken businessmen, were over. It was time to reinvent herself. Although by no means a maternal type, she had found herself fantasising about large suburban houses, with one or two children (if absolutely necessary) and a doting, well-heeled husband furnishing her with compliments and jewellery in equal measure.

"I've done my bit as an independent woman" she would tell herself. "The deck is still stacked against us massively in favour of men. Why don't I just roll with it?"

By this time, she had arrived at the Piccadilly Line platform and was thankful to see a tube train approaching immediately. Flashbacks to the Tokyo underground that she had become so used to sprang to mind. Their trains were cleaner, quieter, and actually ran to rigid timetables whereas the schedule of trains on the London Underground seemed to owe its operation to a random number generator. There was one advantage though in London. She could get on any carriage she liked. There had been so much trouble with the roving hands of Japanese men on their underground system that the train companies had started running "women only "carriages to avoid the problem.

Penny wedged her case in the luggage space on the train and sat down next to it with a steadying hand preventing it from skittling unwary commuters on their way to work. It was six stops to Northfields station. Each stop had further stuffed the train with people on their way to work and she had to make a lot of fuss to get herself and her pink case off the train before the doors hissed shut. As she watched the back of the train leave the station a lot of memories flooded back to her. This was the station she used to get on to go to school. Shaking her head, as if to dispel the memories to another place, she headed towards the stairs, pretty sure they hadn't installed an elevator since she last used the station and dragged her luggage to the street level where a dishevelled, disinterested tube worker waited to collect her ticket.

As she emerged, she realised that she would have to shake her head a whole lot harder to totally remove the adolescent memories that besieged her. Tawdry looking shops and a litter strewn street seemed hardly to have changed in 15 years and Penny couldn't avoid the feeling that she had somehow been skating over a frozen lake for the years since she was last there and now the ice was melting, and she was being inexorably drawn back into its murky depths.

Her destination was only two streets away and even in her ungainly high heels, and with a large suitcase trailing behind her it wasn't long before she was facing a dilapidated red door. The paint was peeling on parts of it to reveal the original light blue colour and some leaflets from a local double-glazing firm protruded from the letter box like a pocket handkerchief on a man's blazer.

Opening her bag, she pulled out her purse and fished inside a zipped compartment which held a single Yale key. For a moment, she paused, key in hand, as if she still had a chance to change her mind, but then submitting to the inevitable, she inserted the key in the well-used lock and entered the house.

A transistor radio was blaring from the back of the house and as Penny slammed the door shut behind her the volume was immediately reduced and a voice shouted, "who's there?"

"It's me mum, Rita. I'm back home. Stick the kettle on."

As a battered old kettle was filled and placed on a gas hob in Northfields, seven miles west John was approaching his cab. Having become accustomed to the bowing and scraping involved with high class hotels and Business class travel a part of him was expecting the cab driver to be waiting with the back door open, ready to whisk him safely into the passenger seat, away from the snow whilst taking care of his luggage. Delroy had condescended to lower his front window an inch. "Come on mate, it's freezing!" John resignedly opened the back door himself and threw his luggage in, slamming the door after him.

"Good trip?" Delroy shouted over his shoulder.

"Fucking place is a zoo. People all over the place...even at 2.00 a.m. in the morning. I've eaten some crap food too. Geezers eating dried fish at lunchtime and then standing on the toilet seats when they have a dump. I'm not putting my hand up for that anymore."

Delroy chuckled to himself as he pictured his back seat customer trying to adapt to any practices that weren't dyed-in-the-wool British. "They say travel broadens the mind, John!"

"Who does? "replied John "Travel agents I bet".

John was trying to signal he'd had enough of conversation. He considered his new status as a jet set traveller meant he shouldn't indulge in gossip with the menial classes and the affront of not having the door opened for him on the cab deserved a little bit of indifference on his part. As if to emphasise this he picked up the free copy of the Financial Times he'd been given on the flight and intently studied a page at random of the distinctive pink broadsheet. He was aware he may have to resume communications at the end of the journey when he needed to restock his white powder reserves but until then he would "punish" his driver a bit.

Far from feeling snubbed, his driver took the chance to try out a new selection cassette he'd just finished recording at home. "George Duke "was the felt tip name written on the case and as he one-handedly navigated the roundabout outside Heathrow whilst extricating the cassette from its case Delroy managed to edge the volume up a little too, and eagerly anticipate the Latin style percussion and slapped-bass intro of "A Brazilian Love Affair".

The M4 was running quite smoothly into town and although he'd landed early in the morning John would have to go straight to work. The downside of his bank paying for business class flights was that they expected you to be able to sleep comfortably on the flight and therefore come straight to work. John had already got bored with the FT and was conscious of the fact that with the increased noise of the cab at motorway speeds the volume of the sound system had been edged up too. As he was not talking to Delroy, he decided not to say anything. His mind wandered to the past week and all that had happened. Like all successful traders, he could easily forget about his failures and give much weight in his mind to his successes. The indignity of Roger Forsyth's practical joke had taken a little longer than most things to fade in his memory but now he was wholly concentrating on the willowy dancer he had met in the lounge at Heathrow. He could see her on his arm at the ceaseless rounds of society parties that he was doubtless going to be involved in as he climbed higher in the social ranking of capital markets. Gazing dreamily out of the cab window he saw a tube train on a bridge over the motorway, little knowing the object of his affections had been on that very line 30 minutes earlier. Had he been able to see a little further he would have been encouraged by the sight of Penelope, gracefully dipping a

Rich Tea biscuit in a large mug of tea, studying his card, flat on the table in front of her.

"What you got there?" Her mother's harsh voice interrupted her thoughts.

"Some guy I met at the airport, thinking of calling him, but don't want to look to keen." Penelope cupped her mug of tea.

"Why didn't you give him your number?"

"That's not how it's done these days Mum."

Penelope was being less than truthful in this response. She felt that to reveal to people she was Rita from Northfields was something she was not yet ready for, and therefore any clues to her background had to be carefully hidden. For the moment Penelope was mysterious and enigmatic to John, and it would certainly remain that way for some time. She resolved to call him in a couple of weeks...and as if to prevent herself from doing it too early, she placed the card carefully in the zip pocket inside her purse that she had recovered her front door key from.

"I'm going to bed mum...didn't get much sleep on the plane. "

As she passed her pink case at the bottom of the stairs a thought crossed her mind. Carefully laying it down flat and dialling in the correct combination, she reached into its depths and tugged on a plastic bag between numerous sets of lacey underwear.

"I got you something from Tokyo mum".

Penelope thought her Mum's smile to welcome 200 Marlboro Lights was slightly wider than the one that greeted her arrival, but she was happy anyway.

"Thanks babe, what time you want me to wake you up?"

"Just leave me.... I feel I could sleep for a week".

CHAPTER 17

T he high-pitched squeal of the taxi's brakes raised John from his fitful dozing in the back of the cab. Business class seats notwithstanding, he hadn't slept well on the inbound flight and was not looking forward to a day clinging on to his shiny leather chair. As he prepared to alight it occurred to him that maybe a couple of bags of Delroy's finest might help him make it through the day. Poking a handful of cash through the sliding glass dividing screen behind the driver he almost whispered "and a couple of bags please mate".

An exchange of this type directly outside his office may have seemed unduly brazen to many people, but one of the advantages of the Black cab cover was that it looked the most natural thing in the world for a customer to pass his payment through the screen and to receive an invoice back from the driver. With such bad weather outside it was much more likely than leaning through the passenger side window to do it. Also, with the snow, John was pretty sure the chances of a casual onlooker seeing anything unusual going on were pretty close to zero.

As he hefted his case out of the cab, still slightly miffed at Delroy's complete refusal to come even close to leaving his driving seat, he thought about how nice it was to be back in his element. He had massively enjoyed priority travel, and the sophisticated hotel, but he would have to try to find a business trip in future where the necessity to do any work was much reduced. He pulled his case through the slush in front of his bank's main entrance and made his way over to the lifts.

The dealing room was well into its daily routine by the time John reached his desk. A few people who weren't on the phone acknowledged his return but generally his colleagues were intent on the screens in front of them. Rupert was also on the phone as John walked past the glass partition of his office. A hand was raised in greeting as he nestled the phone on his shoulder whilst shuffling papers with the other hand. John waved back and made his way to his seat. He flicked his screens on, pressed a button and hollered down the microphone "Grub, I'm back mate. What's been going on?"

If Fieldy was expecting an in-depth summary of major market moving occurrences in London during his week in Hong Kong, he would have been disappointed. He wasn't.

There was a short pause before he got a response. "Did you hear about Patrick's knob?"

John quickly picked up his handset and transferred the call away from the speaker. Even someone as insensitive as he was realised some subjects were not meant to be broadcast all around the trading floor.

Markets were slow, and the day seemed like a week to John. The pick-me up he'd got from Delroy was a wise precaution, and after a mid-afternoon visit to the gents he was even considering going out that night. Wisdom got the better of him and he decided to go straight home.

Across town someone else was deciding whether to go out that night too. Monday night was probably the only night that Robbo would dismiss as a potential drinking opportunity, but he knew Ana was working that night and hadn't seen her for almost five days. He felt mightily flattered by the fact she had given him her home telephone number recently, and felt it proved to those of his colleagues who poured scorn on his relationship that he was getting closer to her.

He removed the pocket diary and opened it on the page where she had written it down for him with the imprint of her ruby red lipstick identifying it as hers. It must have been at least 10 minutes of him staring at the number, weighing up whether he was being too smothering by calling her, before he started tapping out the numbers on his keypad. As soon as it started ringing, he stood up, away from his desk stretching the coiled lead on his handset to its maximum distance. He was on the point of hanging up when Ana finally answered. "Ola?". Robbo loved her speaking in Portuguese and after 30 odd years of life finally found himself wishing he could speak a foreign language (something he had thought totally unnecessary up to this point).

"Hi Ana, it's Robbo. You working tonight? I came in Friday, and they said you was off sick. How are you now?"

The subdued tones Robbo was speaking in made Ana doubt at first that it was really him, but after putting two and two together, and reasoning that Robbo would probably not want his conversation with a stripper to be overheard by colleagues, she answered him.

"I'm still sick meu querido. Why don't you come around to me tonight? I have something to tell you."

Robbo could hardly contain his excitement. Their meetings had been confined to the club that she worked at or Hotel rooms that Robbo had hired out. He had a mate who worked on the night desk at the Tower Hotel. For a cash payment you could get a room for as short a time as you needed it without it needing to be recorded or appearing on credit cards. It was for this reason it became known amongst his mates as "Tower by the Hour".

"Just give me your address babe and I'll be round about 5.30".

Robbo faithfully copied down her details under the lipstick marked number and after saying his goodbyes started thinking whether he should turn up with some chocolates or flowers.

As he placed the diary back in his pocket his mind started racing ahead to the implications of this new milestone. Obviously, he'd have to stop her doing the stripping. Can't be introducing her to mates who had seen her stark naked on a regular basis. Robbo glossed over these considerations. Surely, she would love to be on the firm with him? That's what women want don't they? A geezer to look after them. His imagination was running wild as he conjured up the expressions on the faces of some of his mates back home when they saw how fit she was.

He was decided...flowers **and** chocolates. Ordering the flowers was simple, but once again, with his macho man image in the office to maintain he found himself talking even more quietly to the florists than on his previous call. After two attempts to read out a suitably lovey-dovey message for the accompanying card at a level that the florist would have had to have the hearing of a bat to understand, his voice returned to normal dealing room levels "fuck it, I'll come down there and write it myself!"

Bashing the phone down he tilted his chair back and stuck his heels on the desk in front of him. Onlookers would have seen a serene smile spreading across his chubby features as he pictured her face when he turned up at her door bearing gifts.

In a top floor flat in Islington Ana's face had nowhere near the same serenity. Flowers and chocolates were far from her mind as she gripped onto the side of her florid purple toilet pan and once again retched into it. She knew the reason she was being sick, in fact had expected it if the truth be told. It didn't mean you suffered any less though. Tonight's meeting was going to be tough, but absolutely necessary. She needed to do some stuff around the place before Robbo turned up and hoped that at some point, she could get far enough away from the toilet to make the place look a little less salubrious. Ana guessed that Sonia, the Italian stripper she shared the flat with, would have suspicions as to the reason behind her sickness, but if she did, she hadn't said anything yet. She worked the same clubs as Ana and was due on at 5 p.m. that night so Ana would have the flat to herself for Robbo's visit. Standing up straight, and sipping at a glass of water, she caught sight of herself in the long mirror on the bathroom wall. She took the time to study intensely the reflection she saw. Had she changed much in the last weeks? Her stomach still looked board flat, as it had when she was at the height of her athletics. She still ran most days, often along the canal towpaths around her home. As if to reassure herself she passed her hand lightly over her stomach, perhaps wondering if she could feel something with her fingers that the eye could not see. Continuing her status check she slid her hand under the crop top she was wearing and cupped a breast. "Nope, no change there" she thought to herself. As she spun around to check her rear in the mirror another wave of nausea overcame her, and Ana was once again on her knees. She hadn't felt this bad since she broke her secondary school's 400m record.

Thankfully by the time there was a cheery "rat-a-tat" on her front door she had recovered enough to apply a little make up and put some track suit bottoms on. As she went up on tip toes to reach the spyhole in the door, a large bunch of roses was all she could see. With a mixture of happiness and trepidation she swung the door open to let Frank almost leap through, decapitating three rose heads on the door frame and denting a large Godiva box in his eagerness to enter. Ana gestured with her left hand..." go in the front room".

As Frank sank his substantial bulk into the well-worn three-seater sofa he was already aware that Ana was troubled.

"You ok? Wassamatter?"

Ana had considered many different ways of telling Frank but finally just spat it out.

"I'm pregnant."

It was Ana's turn to think that Frank's demeanour was not its usual self.

After what seemed like ages, but was probably only seconds, the first thing Frank could think of was perhaps not what Ana was expecting. "who's is it then?"

Again, Frank experienced a look on Ana's face that he hadn't seen before. Anger this time. Her eyes flashed darkly at him. "Who do you fuck think?"

Normally he would have teased her at her improper usage of English swear words, but the situation had his mind racing and in the subsequent silence he experienced the opposite of a man falling out of a window. Rather than his past life flashing before him it was the future, with multiple options that he saw. Some appealing and some downright scary. By the time his crystal ball had stopped revolving he noticed Ana had stomped out into the kitchen. Extricating himself from the clutches of the sofa he followed her there and suddenly realised that all he had done was think of himself and the implications for him. Ana was standing by the sink gazing out of the window at the backs of the Victorian houses that made up most of her local area. As he sidled up behind her and put his arms around her, he whispered in her ear. "Don't worry about nothing. I'll take care of you and the sprog"

As she turned, he was able to see her cheeks wet from tears and as she reciprocated his embrace a wave of almost paternal affection swept over him. They stayed like that for some time until Frank, feeling somewhat uncomfortable now about all this emotion, disengaged himself from her arms and wandered over to the fridge. "We got to celebrate now. Got any shampoo? It'll go lovely with them chocolates".

CHAPTER 18

C hopper was less than happy. The bonus round had come and gone, and the unwritten message had been received loud and clear. He'd got the proverbial "goose egg", nothing, nada, zilch. Whilst his salary was generous, he tended to live fully to it. He also felt a bit insulted. Some of those loser salespeople were getting something, he was sure. It was time to move on. He needed somewhere that appreciated his talent. To this end he'd put some feelers out a week or so after the bonus round and told a couple of head-hunters. He'd been hearing some stories lately about the size of some fixed contract deals being handed out on the street and was sure he could lock himself into one of them with a bit of luck. He knew Rupert was being somewhat kind to him. Normal form in the City was unceremonious. You were given your marching orders, and after clearing your desk out you were escorted out of the office within the day. The upside was that you normally had at least a month's notice or "gardening leave ". Rupert had effectively given Chopper his notice with the zero-bonus award, the implication was that he was being given some time to find a job...getting a job was always easier and paid much better if the hiring house had to "prise" you out of your existing post, so Rupert had done him a favour. Chopper did not see any massive upside in taking on new positions so resolved to spend more time down the "battle cruiser" (boozer) in the afternoons. Having had a few first interviews Chopper was confident they would soon be beating a path to his doorway to compete for his signature.

In the meantime, it was important to keep your network going. That's what he told his long-suffering wife anyway. "It's not what you know, it's who you know". Chopper liked dispensing home spun wisdoms, particularly whilst tapping the side of his nose with his finger. It was an interesting situation that his position, although supposedly strictly between him and Regal Bank, meant brokers were very keen to take him out so that wherever he turned up they would have a good shot at his business.

In a massive display of self-restraint Chopper had decided that even by his standards he'd been hitting it a bit hard over the last couple of weeks so when a couple of old mates in the forex markets asked him out for a couple of beers and a steak sandwich on Friday, he thought it was a better option than the full sit-down banquets that had become customary. As he rose from his chair and started putting his jacket on Fieldy looked up momentarily from his phone call. "See ya Monday Chop".

"Na, na…I should be back, only a light one today" Chopper protested.

Fieldy's look needed no words and he returned to his conversation as Chopper ambled over to the coat hooks to put his raincoat on.

The three arms of financial markets all seemed to have different characteristics, equities mostly the domain of the upper echelons of society, foreign exchange the financial equivalent of an East End street market and capital markets coming somewhere in-between. Chopper's two foreign exchange mates fitted right into this generalisation, and he also felt they operated at a much higher volume than most normal people. After a high decibel greeting at the bar, they pulled up three stools and started demolishing Steinlagers for no better reason than the barman was from New Zealand. With their frequent swearing and volume of conversation it wasn't long before there was a virtual exclusion zone around them rather like a penicillin blob in a bacteria filled petri dish.

The three friends were oblivious to what was going on around them and whilst the two traders came from the same part of town as Chopper, by 1.45 p.m. they were only understanding every third word. Having managed to convey to the barman that they wanted the bill he handed it to them and said, "you guys have had a fair drink".

"Why's that?" responded one of the forex boys.

"36 Steinlagers is a fair lunch, even in New Zealand!"

The three of them found this rather amusing and were still laughing as they made their way over to the door of the restaurant. After three tries to pull the door open Chopper suddenly saw the light (and the "Push" sign) and barrelled through the door out onto the street.

The scene that greeted them was of a biblical downpour, Taxis aquaplaning through puddles depositing bow-waves of rainwater onto any unfortunate pedestrians stupid enough to get anywhere near the kerb. No words were exchanged, a look and a quick nod of the head towards the restaurant meant a communal decision had been made...back for a few more jars. The barman had witnessed the scene from his vantage point and by the time they reached their still unmoved bar stools three freshly uncapped green bottles awaited them on the bar.

"Thought you normally moved onto the ports after lunch Chopper" announced one of the forex traders, seemingly to everyone left in the bar.

"Nah, nah, no stickies today, got to be sensible. I'm going back to the office after this as I wanna sober up a bit, have a couple of coffees" was the slurred response.

This was greeted by a mixture of laughter and incredulity.

"Wassamatta? Got to take 'er indoors out tonight?"

With a cautionary look to both sides Chopper leaned in towards his drinking companions indicating something of great import was about to be revealed.

"I've got a second interview with the bacons tonight at 5.30."

Even for two forex traders, on the wrong side of 13 beers each, this caused a momentary pause. After a derisory attempt to keep straight faces, which lasted perhaps two seconds, they simultaneously broke into uncontrollable laughter with one losing his breath and the other wiping tears away. It was some time before either could form a sentence.

"Fuck me, I'd give a few bob for a video of that interview...you got to see a Japanese geezer?"

The question was posed by the Forex trader who was thankfully au fait with Chopper's mockney slang for Japanese people. His hands were still on his knees, and he was bent forward trying to regain his breath.

Attempting to get a bit of respect back Chopper replied "Mr Watanabe, I guess he aint Irish"

The third member of the group had now regained enough composure to contribute to the conversation. "You have another couple of beers, and it'll sound like you're talking Japanese!"

With such a copious amount of beer in them his two critics decided they need to go to the washrooms at the same time. Despite his alcoholic mist, Chopper had a fair guess what would be going on in the cubicles and was sure they'd come out wiping their noses. He had never really been an advocate of the white powder and was quite happy with alcohol as his drug of choice. This, and the fact that they seemed to think his second interview was a bad idea, persuaded him to take advantage of their absence. "Drop a shoulder son" he said to himself and staggered over to the exit, glad to see the downpour had eased.

Whilst the rain was lighter, his suit was still a little bedraggled by the time he reached the office. His reappearance on a Friday afternoon was a source of much curiosity to most of the trading floor but to a man they all avoided engaging in conversation with him because,

a) deciphering it would necessitate everything being repeated twice.

b) everyone knew he was a condemned man...guilt by association.

The trading floor adopted the same rules as you would with the charity sellers on the streets:

"Whatever you do, don't make eye contact".

Chopper himself thought he'd been quite smart leaving when he did and decided it was time to start his hi-tech sobering up program. He considered he'd covered up his inebriated state quite well on his walk to and from the coffee machine at the end of the room. To a casual observer (or the rest of the trading floor) it looked more like the legendary Charles Blondin trying to cross Niagara Falls on a high wire. Chopper couldn't work out for the life of him why he only seemed to have a third of a cup when he reached his desk and decided he must have pressed the "espresso" button.

Two more "espressos" and he was starting to think things were going to go well tonight. Japanese banks were reputed to have guys in charge who didn't really know too much about Eurobonds and are just sent over to keep an eye on the Gaijin (outsiders). Chopper was sure he could baffle Mr Watanabe with his specialist knowledge and getting a job offer would surely be a formality.

With increasing optimism, he set out from Regal Bank in good time and was asked by the receptionist to wait for Mr Watanabe on the comfy seats in the glass enclosed atrium on the ground floor. His wait was not long, and he saw a tall, gaunt Japanese man board the escalator down from the mezzanine floor that protruded out over the reception desk. Guessing this was his man Chopper decided to begin getting up. The sofas were perhaps a little too comfy and it turned out to be a good thing that he had commenced the operation whilst the guy was at the top of the stairs. By the time the Japanese man was at the bottom of the escalator Chopper was finally upright and moved towards him extending his hand in greeting.

Mr Watanabe declined the hand and in a very formal traditional Japanese way, with his fingers lined up with the seams of his trousers executed a curt bow towards Chopper and said "Harris-San. Good evening, please come with me.

Chopper was led over to the "up" escalator, thankful that Mr Watanabe was in front, so as not to witness his attempt to board the moving walkway. Fortune smiled on him and with a little hop he successfully negotiated both the bottom and the top of the escalator and followed his interviewer into an office at the other side of the floor. If Mr Watanabe had noticed Chopper's wrinkled suit or smelled his breath he didn't seem to have reacted in any way and the pair finally settled either side of a large highly polished desk with a stack of papers on one side and a telephone keyboard on the other. Looking around the office Chopper decided it was time to break the ice and spotting a large, gaudily coloured papier mâché head with one eye painted in and the other blank on the middle shelf behind Mr Watanabe he ventured, "is he winking at me?"

Mr Watanabe did not look around, nor did he quite understand the question. He knew his English could be better, but he was sure the closest thing he'd heard to the that verb was something to do with masturbation. Deciding to ignore the question, he was sure where the enquiry was pointed and decided to explain what the figure was.

"This is a traditional Japanese Daruma. At the start of the year, we paint an eye to signify starting our project. At the end of the year, we paint the second eye in to celebrate our good fortune. Do you have any similar tradition?"

After thinking for a second Chopper came back with "well, I like to give up drinking at the start of the year but that doesn't normally last long!"

Once again, the incomprehension was written plain across his face and in leaning forward to increase his chances of comprehension Mr Watanabe caught the whiff of alcohol and coffee that seemed to come from every pore in Chopper's body.

Leaning back again from the unpleasant odour he decided to start asking some questions. In his hands he was holding the applicant's CV. He felt this was a thoroughly unacceptable offering but as some of his Japanese colleagues who had been in London longer than him told him it was all that could be expected.

The first question was always a standard opener.

"Why would you wish to work here?"

Chopper's mouth started to move but try as he might Mr Watanabe could not make head nor tail of what he was hearing and despite a slight lack of confidence in his second language he concluded that the guy was obviously still drunk.

"Chotto Matte kudasai" he lapsed into his native tongue and swiftly followed up with "one moment please."

Chopper looked a little crestfallen, interrupted in what he saw as a faultless spiel about the attractions of a Japanese bank and wondered what was so urgent.

Mr Watanabe swiftly picked up the handset and punched four digits into the keyboard.

"Please pass me to Seki-San".

After a small pause there followed a long spell of Japanese which ended with "Hai! Ima Ima."

On replacing the handset there was a short pause before he spoke again.

"Harris-San, would you please wait one moment?"

For the life of him Chopper couldn't work out what was going on and noticed his interviewer nervously looking through the glass screen of the office towards the escalators. Before long the door behind him opened to let in two suited men, one looking like an ill-disguised sumo wrestler and the other a Slavic looking man with close cropped, military style hair.

The sumo wrestler was senior and first to speak.

"Now go sir please."

Chopper was non-plussed by this outcome and turned back towards the office to see Mr Watanabe now standing behind his chair as if using it as protection.

Another double take at the security men and back at his inquisitor seemed to convince him there was nothing further to be gained and he wearily stood up and slurred "suit yourself mate" over his shoulder as he walked out.

Mr Watanabe decided that maybe he was getting better at understanding this drunken Gaijin's speech but could still not work out why he had asked him to "shoot yourself mate."

CHAPTER 19

The comparison between Northfields and Tokyo could not have been more stark. At first Rita had enjoyed not applying make-up, getting to bed earlier and exercising more, but after a couple of weeks she had decided she needed to be closer to somewhere that could provide a little more stimulation. Working in Tokyo had been lucrative, and she found the more she worked the less opportunities there were to spend money. Tokyo was expensive, but by sharing lodgings and eating at the club, she had accumulated a reasonable war-chest. The next stage in her life was posing a dilemma. Do I find a rich husband, or do I earn my own money? Rita was no dewy-eyed naïf. She had never really "fallen in love" in her life and from observation of the men she had been coming into regular contact with considered herself too smart to ever fully trust anyone from that species.

"I'd settle for someone easy going and a good parent" she would tell herself without admitting to the post-script "and a right few quid".

On other days her mind would turn to the very same customers and think "these guys are all earning fortunes and as far as I can see are not the sharpest tools in the box...why can't I do that?"

Rita's lack of academic achievements was not down to any lack of intelligence but rather more a desire to fit in with the in crowd. At school it was extremely "uncool" to do well in classes and she made studious attempts not to put her hand up and answer questions that she knew the answers to for fear of looking too geeky. She had been smart enough to pick up Japanese from her time in Tokyo and wondered whether that may be a string to her bow with the Japanese banks in the City. The only problem she felt was that with the Japanese chauvinistic society it would be more difficult to earn a significant salary at one of their institutions. She concluded that more research was needed. An expedition to Foyles in Charing Cross Road would provide her with the chance to get a book on Eurobonds (that's what most of the chat in her club had been about), and an excuse to reacquaint herself with John Field...she'd let him stew long enough!

"Mum! You out of the bathroom?". Rita could have looked down the hall to answer her question but that would have meant rolling out of her snug duvet.

"Yes, I'm doing breakfast. You want a sausage?" came the reply from downstairs.

"Nah you're alright...I'll fix something myself later." Rita reluctantly threw back the duvet and headed for the bathroom, where a bewildering array of beauty products awaited her. "I'm going to have a bit of a pampering session...I'll be a while".

The calcium encrusted taps of the bath took some turning and as the bathroom began to fill with steam, she turned around to the transistor radio set standing on the washing machine and selected some fitting music. An excuse to get dressed up was welcome and the whole day would be a break from what had become a monotonous existence even after such a short time. It was maybe presumptuous of her that she could expect John to drop anything he had on to see her that day, but she had an inkling that he was very keen on finding out more about the mysterious Penelope and would brook no obstacle to make it happen.

An hour and a half later, she was fully preened and ready to make the call. Fishing out the business card he'd left with her she carefully placed it on the glass shelf next to her mum's phone in the hall.

Her call was picked up before the second ring, "Regal Bank" said a bored sounding voice at the other end.

Trying desperately to ensure there were no traces of any Northfields twang in her accent she asked to speak to John.

"Can I tell him who's calling?" was the response.

"Yes, its Penelope".

She could imagine the scene as the person put the handset up to their shirt to muffle the call and could still slightly hear them shouting across the room.

"Fieldy! Some bird on line 2 for you"

The response was harder to pick up but if she had been there, she would have heard "who is it? Not some broker?"

The next bit was audible "I dunno, her name's Penelope".

John's response was immediate. His current call was immediately cut as he dived into Penelope's line.

"Hiya, I was hoping you were going to call." Was John's first comment before swiftly putting his hand over the speaker part of his handset to shout across the room. "Alright, I've got it, you can hang up now".

As he took his hand off the mouthpiece again, he decided the conversation was not for general consumption and stood up, walking towards the window with the coiled lead of the handset almost stretched straight in his search for privacy.

"So, what you up to? I want to see you again, but you haven't even given me your number."

"I'm up in town today doing some shopping so I wondered if you wanted to meet up?" Penelope's tone was warm and sophisticated (at least that was what she was aiming for).

"Yes, yes brilliant. Can I take you for lunch?" As John suggested this his mind was in a whirl. First impressions are important. I can't take her to any City haunts. Number one I don't want to see anyone I know and number two most of the places I go to are not sufficiently posh for someone like Penelope.

Thinking on his feet he made a snap decision. "I'll meet you at the Savoy, in the American Bar, you know it? I should be there about 12.15."

Penelope was suitably impressed and was grateful her choice of clothing was fitting for the venue.

"That would be great" she said, trying not to sound too enthusiastic. "I look forward to it!"

With that she hung up and selected one of her fake Chanel handbags she'd picked up in Hong Kong some years ago. "I'm off out Mum, not sure what time I'll be home ". Without waiting for a reply, she went out onto the street tugging the dilapidated front door shut with a slam and setting off to the Underground station. She decided to go to the book shop first but wasn't sure she whether she wanted him to know she was buying books on Eurobonds. "I'll tell him it's a cookbook. That should keep him quiet". She'd have to get a wiggle on to make Foyles and then the Savoy but obviously she'd get there late. Can't be sitting around in the American Bar on your own. It would look like she was still engaged in her old profession!

Clothing choices were also being made on the other side of the City. After talking to Penelope John took a look down at his tie. Survivor of a few boozy lunches a forensic team would have had a field day with it. This was definitely not good enough for a high-end socialite like Penelope. He needed a consultant on this and there was none better than Nicola in his opinion. John didn't want to appear too ignorant but had noticed all the swap traders were "spoons" and they all wore similar ties that seemed programmed to display their label as the narrow part at the back was always going in a different direction to the wider front part.

A simple question to Nicola gave him most of the information he wanted "What's those ties all the knobs on swaps wear called Nic, the ones with the horse and cart on?"

If Nicola was a little perturbed at being interrupted in her phone call by such an unimportant question, she didn't show it. "Hermes John, they're Hermes".

This somehow triggered some recognition for John, and he remembered a shop in the Royal Exchange that sold them. He could get away with an 11.50 a.m. exit, walk down to the Bank Station, get an Hermes tie (without the H as Nicola had pronounced it) and be at the American Bar in good time.

CHAPTER 20

The American Bar at the Savoy was an institution. It was then and had been for years before. Having first opened its doors in 1893 it seemed the passage of time in there somehow stopped in the 1940's. John was sure the cocktail list hadn't changed since then, and the Count Basie style piano playing nailed the era better than any carbon dating test.

As John surveyed the expensive looking drinks menu, he began to wonder what everyone else was doing in here. When you went to lunch in the City you invariably didn't have to guess why matey on the next table was able to afford that vintage wine and half the time you knew them by reputation if not directly. Here he felt a little out of his depth. The City suit and tie code was a lot less in evidence and, to be honest, people seemed a little more relaxed about things.

His eyes were drawn back to the list of concoctions on offer. Whilst he had heard of a few of the names he really didn't know what cocktail he liked and if truth be told he considered them only worthy of women...not a proper man's drink. Salvation appeared at the top of page two. "Vodka Martini" he almost read out loud. "If it's good enough for Roger Moore and Sean Connery it's good enough for me". John wasn't really worried about the taste of it but wanted to make sure he created the right impression.

After watching the barman going back and forth from bottle to bar numerous times, he was slightly underwhelmed by the size of his slim glass with a twist of lemon peel in that the waiter finally placed, with much ceremony, in front of him. After his first sip he decided that the whole scene, Frank Sinatra classics on the piano, refined easy service, sophisticated looking drink in front of him, did not disguise the fact that the drink tasted like petrol. After looking around to see if he was being watched by anyone, he decided to take the chance to down the drink in one and order a beer. As his fingers curled around the glass stem, he was abruptly stopped in his tracks by the appearance of Penelope at the top of the short flight of stairs leading into the bar. John carefully put the drink down and stood up to wave her in. Penelope, after lowering her sunglasses to regard him through natural light, smiled and glided towards him. If anything, John was even more impressed than his first meeting at the airport. She walked in as if she came here regularly and he privately envied the ease with which she seemed to circulate in what was to John a rarefied social stratum. His confidence in her belonging in places like this was further cemented when she ignored the cocktail list, he passed to her and requested a Long Island Iced Tea from a passing waiter.

"What's in the bag?" he asked, eying the plastic bag she'd put down beside her on the couch.

"Oh, just a recipe book. I like to experiment in the kitchen".

John stopped to wonder whether this was a statement laden with sexual overtones but decide it was far too early in their relationship to start down that line. In fact, rather than any sexual chemistry it was the life she represented and her confidence that he found most attractive. If he could have designed a wife to complete the life he aspired to, the outcome wouldn't have been a lot different from her. By the time her tall, ice filled glass arrived John had reached two conclusions:

I'm going to marry her.

I'm having a Long Island Iced Tea next time.

As with their last meeting, conversation flowed freely. Penelope was, by nature of her job, extremely competent at eliciting response from sometimes shy businessmen and was as skilful as any psychologist in encouraging people to talk about themselves. She'd had to do it in two languages in Tokyo so back home it was a breeze. It also helped that John was in no need of help to open up to her.

Two o'clock soon came and with a wistful look at his watch he summoned the bill and made arrangements to meet up again.

"Do you fancy going to see a show or something next week?"

"That would be great. What are you thinking?" Penelope questioned."

"I'll have a think about it and call you. Can I have your number?"

For the first time he saw just a fleeting uncertainty in her demeanour. "My telephone line's not put in yet. I'll call you on the weekend and you can let me know".

If John had any lingering doubts he was soon distracted by the arrival of the bill. He made a big show of getting his American Express card out to pay for it. Looking at the total he was glad that Regal Bank were going to be picking it up rather than him personally. As they rose and headed out to the taxi stand outside his mind was a battlefield of how to say goodbye. In the end he settled on a light kiss on the cheek and a squeeze of bodies as he held onto the (no doubt) expensive aroma of her perfume.

"You going home now?" John asked as her taxi drew up.

"No, off to Knightsbridge". Penelope answered back over her shoulder. "Take care John, speak soon".

As he waved to her head through the receding back window of the cab, he wondered what sophisticated friends she had in places like Knightsbridge. Had he known a bit more he would have realised that there's a Piccadilly Line station there. Very handy for Northfields.

The receding head in the cab had no scruples about the small deception. She knew what he wanted and how to present that aura. She WAS going to Knightsbridge, but not to see a friend. The assumptions he made were his and his alone.

CHAPTER 21

John had to work hard on his return to the office to stop fantasising about the future course of his relationship with Penelope and as the days wore on, he was grateful for the distraction of busy markets and associated social events to keep his focus away from her. He had been looking forward for some time to the annual Dominion Bank Eurobonds in-house lunch and now he was finally walking up the ornate stone staircase of their historic building.

In-house lunches were somewhat traditional and seemed like a status symbol competition between long-established City Institutions for who had the best kitchen and wine cellar. The problem was the tradition seemed designed for well matured bankers who may indulge in one glass of sherry too much from time to time, not juvenile parvenus with a penchant for drug use and drinking games.

Fieldy and the rest of the attendants at this year's gathering certainly fitted into the latter category and as handshakes were exchanged with each new arrival as they stood around the 18ᵗʰ Century walnut veneered dining table the sense of anticipation was palpable.

Casting his face around the group he could recognise and categorise everyone there. He was a trifle surprised to see a couple of brokers in attendance. These treats were supposed to be saved for the alpha participants in the market surely. He didn't really know one of them that well but the other, Veg, he had bumped into numerous times.

Wandering over to Veg, who as usual seemed in a Zen-like state of happiness, he tapped him on the shoulder and shook hands warmly. "Alright Veg? didn't expect to see no brokers here".

"I'm glad to be invited to something where I don't have to expense it!" was the reply.

"Well, if we bat on afterwards, you'll need your credit card then!" John cautioned.

Veg's serene look was untroubled by this warning, and it wasn't long before a grey-haired lady clad in a floral pinafore shuffled in through a connecting door and after clearing her throat at successively louder levels managed to inform everybody it was time to sit down in readiness for the first course. Unlike more refined gatherings the reaction to her summoning was for everyone to take their jackets off and hang them over the back of their seats as if preparing for battle. A momentary look of trepidation passed over the face of the hostess, Mrs Shore. She had ministered the bank's in-house dining events for many years now and had noticed a marked decline in the behaviour of guests over the last five years. What used to be restrained gatherings with serious conversations about technical subjects that she mostly didn't understand had descended into drinking competitions with conversations she understood far too well thank you very much! With a resigned attitude she returned through the side door and told Magda, her young colleague to begin the service.

Having had the same Chef for as long as she could remember Mrs Shore was asked to participate in the search for the replacement when he unexpectedly died of a heart-attack last year. She was sure his liberal use of butter was a contributory factor but was polite enough to keep her opinions to herself. Her input for the new hire was not completely positive but the remainder of the hiring panel were very keen on his "Nouvelle Cuisine" style of cooking which was very "de rigueur" she was informed, and he was soon at home in the kitchen bringing with him various strange gadgets that looked very unlike the previous incumbent's. Her main criticism was the portion size. She for the life of her could not envisage that the plates being produced would satisfy the smallest of statures let alone some of the substantial figures she had witnessed turning up lately. The worst consequence of this was that in the absence of food they seemed to drink more. Mrs Shore had made a habit of keeping Magda back in the kitchen by the time it got to desserts for fear of any unwanted attention.

She consoled herself with the fact that in two years she could take her pension and snapped into action to help Magda with the first course. She sincerely hoped the assembled guests would enjoy their "blue cabbage chilled soup with scallops" offering, but on looking at the dish with what looked like two teaspoons of duck egg emulsion paint with a lonely scallop (why did he use the plural?) beached in the middle she doubted it.

As she expected, the shortfall in rations was more than compensated for by wine. She had expected there would be high consumption, but this lunch was proving to be record breaking and when her final visit to the dining room presented her with one of the guests sitting comatose in a chair and two others speaking to one another without a word of it being intelligible she decided to whisper in her host's ear that he really ought to be terminating things.

To his credit, Bruce, the Dominion Bank employee and host of the lunch, was sober enough to admit that things had probably gone far enough and agreed with her. Mrs Shore scuttled around clearing what she could while Magda (as instructed) cowered behind the kitchen door until all had left. Whilst Bruce was wise enough to know when to stop, others were not as sensible and Mrs Shore marvelled as she looked out of the window down to the front of the building to see four of the party negotiating the steps at the front of the building, one guy being supported between Terry and John and making their way across Moorgate to the nearest pub. They presented a strange group, one staggering, two of them seemed to have inadvertently exchanged jackets during their lunch as the suits they turned up in now looked like blazer and trouser combinations. She shook her head in disbelief and turned to pick up the last of the port glasses.

Down at ground level things weren't going so well. Despite the fresh air, Tony the Deutsche Mark trader was still comatose. Veg decided he was going to call it a day. Several times on recent drinks he had fallen asleep on the train and woken up at Shoeburyness. A couple of times he'd been on the last train, so it meant an expensive cab ride back. He wasn't doing it again he told himself. "it's only 5.p.m.... even if I do fall asleep at least I can get the train back" He stood up abruptly and announced he was going to catch his train. Fieldy did try to say something, but Veg couldn't catch it, and Tony was still comatose. As he reached fresh air again Veg was extremely pleased with himself at his restraint. His pace quickened as he realised a train home was due in in around 15 minutes and he should make it to Fenchurch Street by then.

He made it with plenty of time and as the train pulled into the station, he walked along to his favourite place on the platform studiously avoiding the "slam "doors being thrown open by people obviously in a rush to get off. The train was empty in no time and taking up his usual seat Veg vowed to himself he was not falling asleep this time. He managed to resist for at least 5 minutes but after that his head angled lazily against the window and time sped past. By some miracle his eyes opened just as he saw the sign for "Basildon" slowly sliding past his window. Springing out of his chair like a scalded cat he quickly worked out he should be able to open the door and jump out before the train picked up speed. Without a further thought he flung the old-style door open and leapt for the platform. Despite the slow speed of the train, he was unable to maintain his footing. Pitching forward on his shoulder he rolled forward twice before ending up in a dusty bundle against the back wall of the platform. His finishing position left him on one side, back against the wall, looking at the train that he'd just jumped from. It was only then that he realised his miscalculation. The train had actually been going slowly because it was pulling into the station rather than leaving it as he had assumed. As the rest of the passengers alighted the train in a more traditional manner there were a few eyebrows raised but generally the good folk of Basildon had more things to worry about than the local drunk pulling another stunt. For quite some time he just remained prone, the amount of alcohol in his system numbing any feelings of embarrassment as the weary commuters picked their way around his outstretched body. An old woman dragging a wheeled shopping trolley was one of the few to show compassion. "You ok darling? Need any help?" Unwilling to admit to any discomfort he stood up and assured her he was fine. Dusting himself down he limped to the ticket barrier.

"Well, I didn't miss my stop" he consoled himself.

Back in the City, things were going equally awry for Tony the Deutsche Mark trader. John Field was not someone you wanted in the trenches with you and with

Veg leaving the pub, and Tony unable to communicate, he decided it was time for him to leave too. He was sure Tony would wake up at some time. The comatose trader was stuck on a hidden-away banquette seat at the back of the pub, so it was some time before he was spotted by one of the bar staff collecting glasses. It wasn't long before Tony's complete lack of response prompted an emergency call, and it was even quicker for the ambulance crew to analyse the problem. The decision was taken by the paramedics to take him in to sleep it off and to try to find a next of kin to notify in case things got worse. From his mobile phone inside his jacket, they were able to find a contact labelled "wife" and make the awkward call.

"Hello Mrs Wilson, it's Bart's Hospital here. We have your husband here and he's quite unwell. We thought we should let you know in case you were expecting him."

There was a short pause before a shrill reply. "I knew he'd get pissed today. In-house lunch he says...they're always the worst. I'm getting bloody fed-up with this. Can't you give him something to make him sick?"

"That's not really what we do Madam. I would suggest you come up but that's up to you".

Again, there was hesitation before her response. "OK, but I'll have to park the kids with my Mum first".

It was a good two hours before she made it up to town and after checking at the front desk, she got the lift to the third floor and presented herself at the nurse station.

"I'm here to see Mr Wilson".

She was sure the nurse's look conveyed "oh you're the one with the loser, piss-head husband" but perhaps she was imagining things.

"Certainly Mrs Wilson. Follow me."

The Nurse marched up to the third bed on the left and looked sympathetically at the visitor. "Here you are."

The surprised expression on Karen Wilson's face was not what the nurse was expecting.

"That's not my husband!"

The nurse frantically looked at the bed notes clipped on the end of the bed and then said "Terry Wilson, that's your husband, isn't it?"

"Yes, but that's not Terry Wilson, at least it's not MY Terry Wilson."

"We got your details from his jacket. His wallet had ID and his phone had your number" said the nurse holding up the jacket which had been draped over the chair at the side of the bed.

"That's his jacket, but that isn't him!"

At around the same time Veg had finally made it home. Why were his wife and kids not home?

More importantly, why did his door keys not work?

CHAPTER 22

As the weeks passed the recounting of Veg's exit from the train was relayed and retold around the City until someone else did something stupid worthy of note. The wait was normally not a long one. Fieldy had used the time for another couple of assignations with Penelope and nothing had changed in the feelings he had for her. In fact, he was so sure of himself and proud of her he felt it was time to introduce her to his social circle. Finding the right occasion was the only quandary he had so when Grub suggested one day that he would like to invite him to the Albert Hall to see Frank Sinatra, Sammy Davis Jr and Liza Minelli in concert he immediately piped up "how many tickets you got? Can I bring my bird?"

"Well, we're in a box, there's 8 seats...I think Veg is inviting someone so I'm sure I could squeeze her in. How long you been seeing her you dark horse?"

Fieldy tried to gloss over this question and was very unspecific about exact time scales but assured Grub it was the real deal.

"Wait 'til you see her mate, she's a real keeper".

"What she plays in goal?" Grub always liked teasing traders when he could.

"Very funny" was Fieldy's curt response. "We gonna meet up town for a few drinks first?"

"Yeah, if you want. Any ideas?" Grub didn't often venture past the City limits.

"I'll ask Penelope, she's more up on West End places than us...that's her manor really".

"Lovely mate, got any prices?" Grub thought he may as well use the opportunity to get something out of him while he was on the line. The Sinatra tickets hadn't been cheap and two of them definitely deserved some help.

John duly obliged and quickly reeled off a list of prices before hanging up and immediately pulling a small diary from his inside jacket pocket to look up her telephone number.

He had been enormously encouraged by Penelope deciding to give him her telephone number and he also found out where she was living, although she made it clear she was only there temporarily and would not appreciate any home visits. He'd been a little nonplussed, expecting a Knightsbridge flat or something but wasn't massively worried about it. She answered on the third ring. He wasn't sure it was her on her first response, but she soon regained her recognizable accent and he ploughed on regardless.

"Hi babe, got a big night for you...how you fancy Frank Sinatra and his mates at the Albert Hall in a private box?"

"Not really my bag John, how old is he? I'd be happy to string along though if you'd enjoy it" Penelope sounded much less impressed than he expected.

"He's the nuts babe, you'll love it. I think he aint much over 50...and he's timeless anyway. We were thinking of meeting up somewhere nearby for pre drinks...any ideas?"

With scarcely a pause she replied, "Harvey Nick's, 5th floor".

Fieldy smiled inwardly, his confidence in her West End sophistication restored.

"Ok we'll meet you there after work". He was going to add more but was interrupted by Grub shouting through the box.

"I got something on those sniffers mate".

Sniffers was market parlance for bonds issued by the French Government Guaranteed "Société Nationale des Chemins de Fer" SNCF the French railway system.

In the prices he had given to Grub he had pushed the SNCF up a little higher than the market as it was an issue Nicola had outlined as cheap recently, so he was more inclined to be buying them than selling them.

Picking up the phone to Grub his first comment was "Hope he's a seller".

"He's sizing you up on the bid mate".

Market convention was for people to show bids and offers in certain sizes. In $ markets it could be a $1million x $1million market which meant the price was only good for that size. If someone asked the size on a price, etiquette said he was obliged to trade on it because he had effectively got the person making the price to show their hand.

John was in a particularly ebullient mood. He was going to see one of his long-term idols at the Albert Hall accompanied by his glamourous girlfriend and now someone wanted to hit him in a bunch of bonds he thought were nice and cheap (he trusted Nicola implicitly).

He wondered if he could get as many as $10million, then he could show the block to one of her customers.

"How many you want to buy like that mate? I think he's got good size" Grub asked.

John was immediately aggressive at the suggestion he couldn't stand up to the other counterparty's size. "How many's my bid for Grub"? He continued in a sarcastic tone. "Let's put it this way. How many fishes are there in the sea? How many stars in the sky?" At the other end of the line Grub thought this was stunningly arrogant, even for Fieldy.

"I can't fucking tell him that can I, why don't you just say a number?" Grub sounded panicked.

"His size is my size" was Fieldy 's terse reply.

Hanging up the phone he eagerly awaited the response back from Grub and shouted over to Nicola "Oi! I may be getting some of those sniffers you like Nic".

She was on the phone, a fact completely ignored by Fieldy, but managed to raise a thumb in acknowledgement.

"John, pick me up" Grub's voiced sounded very surreptitious over the box and Fieldy wondered what he needed to say that couldn't be said over the box.

"Whassup?"

Grub cleared his throat before saying anything "$130 million you get!"

Fieldy looked as if he'd been hit by a bus. The colour drained from his face as he digested what he'd just heard.

Grub had waited long enough. "Are we done?"

"That's about 65% of the whole fucking issue. I can't do that." His voice was quivering as were other parts of his body.

"Well, the seller's telling me we're done. His express words were "I studied astronomy at university, and it is believed there are between 100 billion and 400 billion stars in the galaxy so 130 million should be fine."

"It doesn't matter" John argued back, "I can't write that ticket. Line's out." He smashed the phone down on the desk chipping small piece of plastic from the earpiece which narrowly missed a colleague next to him.

He could still hear Grub through the speaker "I've got to get this done mate; he's holding me to it".

John turned the speaker off too and stood up to clear his head. As he wandered aimlessly around the dealing room, trying to focus his thoughts, his eyes alighted on Nicola, now off the phone, looking intently at her Bloomberg screen. Suddenly the fear was momentarily replaced by the other side of the City's ying and yang forces...greed.

"If I got a block of these sniffers, you reckon you could sell 'em?"

"I'm pretty sure I could John" Nicola was starting to make him feel a whole lot better.

"How many"

"Probably as many as $10 million". Nicola was somewhat surprised at the reaction to this and without a word John petulantly stalked back to his desk. Fear had swiftly reasserted itself.

Frank Sinatra was the furthest thing from his mind on his way home that night.

CHAPTER 23

O ver at Plummers, Grub's normally self-assured manner was visibly absent to his colleagues. It was part of a broker's armoury to be aware of trades going on around you, so it wasn't long before most of the room were aware of the incident. After some attempted cajoling with the seller of the bonds he threw his handset against the screen, ran through a few expletives and then thrust himself away from the desk on the wheels of his chair before lumbering to his feet and heading over to Kevin Conolly's office. The fact they'd grown up together on the same council estate meant he dispensed with the formality of knocking and burst straight in.

"We got a massive problem Kev. Fieldy's hooked me on a trade and the seller's trying to stick me to it."

"'Ow many?" Kevin's East End lack of H's was even more noticeable than Grub's.

"$130 million!"

There was silence for a moment as Kevin considered things. He never told anyone, but his first thought was not about being stuck with a position but how much brokerage

Plummers would clear on the trade. As he rubbed his stubbled chin Grub was sure he noticed in Kev's eyes that a decision had been reached.

"I'm gonna talk to his boss Rupert. He's a decent bloke. Has he said anything yet? I suppose silly bollocks Fieldy has dropped off the radar?"

"Yeah" replied Grub. "I've tried him on the outside line too and he's just ignoring me".

"Leave it to me mate, and by the way, aint that cheeky fucker being taken to the Albert Hall by you in a couple of weeks?"

"I invited him just this morning" admitted Grub. "And his treacle"

"Well, he can stick that right where the sun don't shine if I don't get this sorted out".

Kevin started looking through an old box of business cards for Rupert De Villiers' direct line and as he was doing it he continued to bark out instructions.

"Go and pull the tapes as well mate, make sure we're all clean as a whistle. Not that I don't trust you, but this has to be bang to rights."

All trading calls were recorded downstairs on large reel to reel tape recorders so as to make any disputes about prices or sizes easily resolved.

Grub wandered off to the fire escape staircase at the side of the dealing room to descend to the back-office with its gargantuan tape machines and Kevin finally found the card he was looking for.

He had known Rupert for quite some time and covered him as a broker in the early years. If he had photographs of some of the nights out they'd had together he could probably blackmail him into accepting the trade he thought, but in Kevin's estimation Rupert had been one of the more genuine guys he'd met in the City. He was sure that with the chance to explain things he could smooth this out.

He stabbed the numbers from the card into the keyboard in front of him and waited three rings before a cultured voice at the other end answered. "Rupert De Villiers".

"'Ello mate, long time no speak. It's Kev, how's it going?"

"Too big and important to talk to me now are you?" Rupert teased.

"Thought it was the other way round geezer! Listen can I buy you a quick beer tonight? There's something I need to sort out urgently. Have you talked to Fieldy?"

"Not since lunchtime, what's the problem?"

Kevin told him it was something best discussed face to face and they agreed to meet at an equidistant bar at 5.30.

"I'm not up for a session like the old days though...got to act with some constraint now".

Rupert's liver was already going into contortions at the thought of replicating some of the benders they had been on in the past.

"Don't worry about that, this is a subject for sober heads". Kevin's sombre tone made Rupert very curious about what grave subject could stand between Kevin Connolly and a bucketful of lager but decided he could wait until 5.30 p.m. to find out.

Rupert got to the bar on the dot, but as he arrived, he saw the familiar figure of Kevin there already in an elegant dark suit with expensive looking cufflinks peeking out from the sleeves of his jacket.

The two shook hands warmly, had it been one of his old friends from the East End he might have gone in for the full hug but figured Rupert's mob would feel uncomfortable with that sort of thing and restricted himself to a second hand on top of Rupert's right hand.

"I got you a beer. Cheers"

The two clinked bottles and raised them to their mouths before placing them back on the bar before Kevin indicated a secluded corner at the back of the room. "Let's go over there" he indicated.

Rupert's curiosity was pricked even more by the need for such measures but followed obediently.

In the ten minutes or so that followed Kevin carefully outlined the process of events that had transpired that day and even offered to play the recording of the call on a Sony Walkman he had brought along.

Rupert didn't consider this necessary and was shocked that no mention had been made of this before he left the office.

Kevin's estimation of his old friend's moral compass was not unwarranted. The whole process had taken a lot less time than he had imagined to reach a conclusion.

"The trade's done Kev. I'll make sure John tickets it in the morning. I'm not prepared to be any part of an organisation where people don't stand by their word. It's fundamental to the business really".

With the main topic out of the way the conversation turned to catching up on each other's lives and events over the last few years but although Kevin would have seemed quite normal in his interaction with Rupert, at the back of his mind he was scheming. The benefit of cultivating such relationships was not just in the trades he got when he was broking but also in cases like this, where he could call upon senior participants in the market and utilise long-standing relationships for his benefit. This one had certainly come up trumps and in his estimation, he was now in Rupert's debt. As they shook hands at the end of their conversation and wandered homeward a thought occurred to him about a special offer he'd decided to buy in a recent chat with his ticket tout, Bertie Wybrow. Ticket touts were an essential contact for broking firms. A guaranteed supply of front row tickets for prolific traders was the perfect grease to lubricate the wheels of business and Bertie never disappointed. As he was another contact from Kevin's childhood, he could trust him implicitly. This was not a quality that touts were necessarily well known for.

"Two grand mate! Four of youse get a chopper from Battersea to Oxford for a slap-up lunch wiv fancy French cooking. Then back into town for a piss-up at night. That's value. Someone's let me down on it".

Bertie's description of a Helicopter ride to "Le Manoir aux Quat' Saisons" for lunch may have differed somewhat from Raymond Blanc's but Kevin had developed a liking for fine dining, and this seemed too good an opportunity to forego. His only problem after saying "mine" was who to dispense such largesse on. It seemed that dilemma had been resolved, particularly as the brokerage due to be collected on the trade was $39,000.

CHAPTER 24

Rupert made sure he was in early the next morning as he knew he could catch Fieldy before many people arrived. Blissfully unaware, John sauntered in about 10 minutes later and was immediately summoned to the office. From the outset he was struck by how formal Rupert's tone was and it wasn't long before he knew why.

"You can't go around making statements like this. We're in a major financial market, not a poker game. Dictum Meum Pactum". John still remembered enough of his schoolboy Latin to know what this meant. "My word is my bond", the motto of the London Stock Exchange.

"But I would have busted my limits if I bought them".

"I can increase your limits if necessary, which I have done, because you <u>are</u> going to be writing a ticket with Plummers as soon as you walk out of here. Of course, there's always the alternative".

"What's that then"? asked John timidly.

"Don't make such bombastic claims in the first place. Let your brain catch up with your mouth sometimes."

Rupert paused briefly before continuing in a more subdued vein.

"Do you like the bonds? How cheap are they"?

"Well Nicola likes them, and they look cheap to other things, but you have to assume the lead manager has been trying to knock them out without much luck since they were issued".

John's tone was returning a little towards his normal level.

As if to signal an end to the conversation Rupert took a page from a cardboard file and handed it across the desk.

"Here's official notification of your new limits. Remember with bigger limits I expect you to make more money".

"Thanks boss" was all John could find to say and having received the signal loud and clear he carefully folded the piece of paper and returned to his desk. He spent ten minutes or so wondering how to broach his first contact of the morning with Grub before turning the Plummer's box on again and picking up the handset.

"Grub, you there"?

The reply was almost instantaneous.

"Hello mate, how's it going"?

Some people might have expected Grub to have been a little more cantankerous with him for the anguish caused but being a good broker meant, in a lot of cases, a degree of bedside manner worthy of a psychoanalyst. There was little upside in him getting in an argument about the trade, particularly as Kevin had told him it was sorted, and the wildly oscillating moods of some traders meant a straight bat defence was the recommended way of dealing with most of them.

"They like to think they're always right and it don't do no good to remind them when they aint"

was an early piece of advice he had received. A trader once told him "I don't want my broker to have opinions... just prices".

Grub was quite happy to operate on this level. He did have many opinions, but just kept them to himself. The value of maintaining good relationships with anyone from the market making side of the business had been made abundantly clear to him this very day by his boss.

As John read back the trade details down the line, Grub filled in his ticket and once again marvelled at how his old mate had made this all happen so smoothly and quickly. Some people in the office resented how little Kevin seemingly did in his management position compared to how much he earned. In Grub's opinion (which he didn't keep to himself between colleagues) this is exactly what management were there for.

Having finally written the ticket and entered it into the system he thought he would leave a day or so before discussing meeting points for the Albert Hall trip. Fieldy still sounded a bit sheepish so he would leave contact with him to a minimum for now.

CHAPTER 25

Frank emerged breathless from the stairs at Bethnal Green Underground station and cut diagonally through the small park adjoining it. The late spring weather meant it wasn't long before he was putting his jacket over his shoulder and getting rid of his tie. In the two months since Ana's shock revelation a lot had changed for him. He had managed to find a small flat within easy distance of the City and was now covering her rental bill. If anything, he thought she looked even better than when he first saw her. Her tummy, whilst obviously pregnant, seemed like some strange extension added to what was an otherwise flawless body in his mind. She also had a really healthy glow in her eyes that he thought was absent before. There was the possibility that Frank was somewhat biased in his feelings, but they do say beauty is in the eye of the beholder.

Mulberry House was a sprawling, 30's-built block of flats in Victoria Park Square. Entrance was through an impressive arch, but the dwellings were less impressive inside.

The walk from the Underground was mercifully short and his cheery knock on the door was swiftly met by Ana and an aroma of home cooking emanating from within. "Hi Robbo, guess what's for dinner".

He scooped her up in his arms and carried her into the kitchen as if he thought she was the first course.

"Suavemente "she cautioned" remember there are two of us in this body!"

"Sorry" he said, depositing her back to the kitchen floor. "What's cooking?"

"Feijoada" she replied.

The look on his face indicated to her that further explanation was necessary.

"It's like a stew, with beans."

"And dumplings?" Robbo seemed quite excited by the prospect.

It was Ana's turn to look puzzled. It was not a word that came up regularly in East-End strip joints.

"They're round and fluffy and made with Suet".

Her face maintained its curious look, so Robbo decided to elaborate. "Suet, it's the fat off kidneys".

Ana's face finally changed, now a look of disgust passed over her face. For her this just confirmed the mistrust she had of English cuisine.

"There's definitely no kidney fat in my Feijoada. Sit down and see what you think."

Robbo walked through to what the estate agent had termed "living-dining room" and carefully manoeuvred his not insignificant bulk behind a gate-leg table with a plastic tablecloth by the window in anticipation of his stew...dumplings or no dumplings. He was followed in short order by Ana with two steaming bowls and some crusty bread.

Apart from a few appreciative grunts they shared the meal in silence. Robbo couldn't help but feel she had something on her mind but was prepared to wait until she was ready. It was as he was wiping the bowl clean with his third bit of bread that she finally opened up.

"I want to go back to Portugal".

If Robbo had not had a mouthful of bread the resulting silence would probably still have occurred as he processed the information he just heard. He processed the baguette quicker and after some consideration the best he could come up with was "why?"

She took a deep breath, questioning where to start in her checklist of reasons to return.

"This is no place for a baby. I don't want to be stuck here all day while you work. Also, this country is not good for a child. I really don't want it to be English. I have to spend six months indoors in this country and eat shit food, my father has been getting weaker and my mother wants me to return to work with her on our Quinta and I miss my brother and sister".

He was quite taken aback with this litany of reasons and wondered where, in this broadside of complaints, he should start.

"I don't know what a Quinta is, but you shouldn't be working in your condition".

"I'm pregnant Frank, not ill!" Ana seemed quite animated.

"Well, you can't just go wandering off with my baby. Don't I have a say in it?"

Frank was starting to get agitated too.

"It's not as if we're married or anything is it?" she spat at him. "I am not a prisoner here am I?"

Frank quietly thought that prison would be a lot cheaper than the rent he was laying out for her flat but decided throwing that into the discussion would not be beneficial.

"Of course you can go. When you thinking of leaving?"

"I've booked some flights for next Monday".

"I've paid three months' rent on this place" he protested.

"I'm sorry, but I'm desperate. Will you be able to take me to the airport?"

"Dunno depends what time." Frank's mind was still spinning. "So, can I come to see you in Portugal? Bet you've told your Mum all about me".

Ana's face was impassive in response to his question. She was yet to tell her Mum she was pregnant let alone anything about Robbo. In fact, the need to let her parents know was probably ahead of all others on the list she unloaded on him.

"She'd love to meet you" was the best, non-committal answer she could think of.

In the aftermath of Ana's revelation, the pair of them sat there a little too engrossed in their own thoughts to pass much conversation. Robbo's dreams of a little mini-me at football with him, matching Spurs scarves around their necks, singing "yid army" together were suddenly replaced by some foreign little oik with greasy hair supporting Benfica and diving every time he got kicked in a football match. Frank would have admitted he could be a bit xenophobic...if he actually understood what it meant. Things that were his dreams, were Ana's nightmares. They both seemed to think it was a boy. A boy that she vowed would not turn into one of the excuses for a real man that she had so much experience of in her stripping career. "Surely all males are not destined to be like this?" She was determined that her son would be raised differently and away from the toxic influences of the City.

Frank decided he felt under pressure deciding things in her presence and squeezed out of his corner seat towards the door." I've got a mate who's a cabbie, if I can't take you to Stansted, he will".

"I'm going down the pub, I need some time alone. G'is us a kiss then"

Ana rose gracefully from an old sofa that was threatening to engulf her and gave him a small peck on the cheek. A far cry from her usual amorous embraces.".

"Fuck me" he thought to himself, "she's leaving and I'm still in the doghouse".

As he exited Mulberry House he knew where he needed to go to think; the nearest pub. The Arabian was just up the road. Two storeys of strippers on the corner of Cambridge Heath Road and Bishop's Way. He wanted to think though, and he knew in such a place he wouldn't be working much out at all. The Greyhound, lively on a weekend night but not alluring right now. It had to be The Dundee .... a run-down old man's pub where he could get a decent pint of Guinness and think things over. He had no idea why he considered Guinness a thinking drink, but likely the whole experience, waiting for the barman to fill the final third of the pint and etching a shamrock on top in the head if you were lucky, elongated the experience. With the glistening black glass in his hand, he carefully went over to the side of the pub between the dartboard and the bar billiards table and sunk into a moth eaten, smoke engrained, sofa.

And he thought.

CHAPTER 26

Delroy was doing some thinking too. He was due to take Grub and Fieldy up west to Harvey Nichols next week as they were going to a concert at the Albert Hall. He was surprised to hear who was playing there and after the booking he decided it was too long since he'd listened to a bit of Francis Albert and started hunting through some old cassette boxes back at the flat. Generally, he felt sorry for white people. They just didn't seem to appreciate music and when he saw some of them dance, he was sure they were listening to a different tune. Once again, he mentally slapped himself for generalising about any race of people. Two Jewish blokes wrote the iconic Libretto Porgy and Bess for God's sake. Gil Evans and Miles Davis's recording of that was amongst his favourite albums. Music was an art; painting, sculpture, poetry were all arts too, but nothing could move him like music or be so evocative of a time or a place. Whoever produced it, the sound of it was the only thing that mattered, not the colour of their skin.

He could remember reading how Sinatra started off as a Bing Crosby style crooner, but with the help of a band leader named Tommy Dorsey he learnt to hold his breath longer and was able to run phrases behind the music giving him a unique sound. By the time he left Dorsey and teamed up with Nelson Riddle he was the finished article and with Riddle's arrangements, they were a match made in heaven. As was common with Delroy, he spent a small amount of time wondering why so many Big Band Leaders in the 40's were trombonists, Dorsey, Riddle, Miller, even going back as far as Kid Ory, but being unable to find any logical reasons he was soon on to sorting out some tunes for the next week or so.

"The Capitol Years" was written in felt-tip pen on the spine of a cassette case. "Gotcha" said Delroy to himself. For him this was the peak of Sinatra's performances. His range still good enough for all the high notes and great orchestrations helping it all along. He'd just come back from midweek football training, so he was in the right mood to relax the body and stimulate the senses. A journey to the fridge provided him with a couple of patties and a glass of milk which he took up to bed along with a large pair of studio grade headphones. He liked to listen to music loud. Midweek in the flats is not the place to be pumping up the volume after 10 pm so this was his indulgent pleasure. Plumping up the pillows he reached across to push the jack plug into the headphones socket and hit play. Who would have thought of a bass clarinet on the intro to "I've got you under my skin"? Nelson Riddle did. Delroy settled back into the pillows and felt a warm blanket of sound fill his ears.

For quite some time he sat like this, listening to the music intently, trying to follow single instruments from the band, almost like isolating a single ingredient in gourmet food, only opening his eyes to reach for another bite of his snack. The third time he did this he was suddenly aware of a change in his surroundings. He could see the reflection of a blue flashing light on his ceiling and on removing his headphones the all too familiar wail of sirens became audible. Placing his headphones on the bedside table he wandered over to the window. His first thought was his lock up, but the action was in the other direction. From his third-floor vantage point the whole "square" was laid out like a relief map to him. The "square" was a pedestrianised area with a few basic shops for the use of the estate. Launderette, butchers, etc. At this time of night, a variety of metal shutters were all in place showing mixed graffiti and a threat to the latest "grass" to have been outed.

The square was where he had hung out as a young teenager, sometimes comparing ball-juggling skills with his mates or other times repelling visitors from other estates trying to assert their strength. It was here he first clashed with Andy O'Brien. Two roads headed into the square, one from each side that both terminated in a blocked end. Both blocked ends were now occupied by patrol cars with blue lights and orange indicators both flashing. The two groups of police men were converging on a small group of teenagers with what looked like an over optimistic hope of catching them. The heavily built cops were no match for the nimble group, some of whom were on small BMXs, and the many pedestrian exits from the shopping centre provided a multitude of escape routes. Delroy's eyes caught some motion in his peripheral vision, and he turned his head slightly to see another three youths at one of the patrol cars. The police had made the mistake of leaving their car doors open in their haste to corral the group of youngsters and in a perfectly executed deception operation, three of the group that had been hiding by the lifts emerged to primarily jump on the bonnet of the car, kicking in the windscreen in and ripping the aerial off. Next, wisely standing some distance away, one of the party chucked a petrol bomb in the driver's door before hastily beating a retreat back into the depths of the estate.

Delroy couldn't help but feel a little nostalgic. Most people round here hated the Old Bill, and whilst the majority didn't advocate petrol bombing their cars, it was unlikely anybody was going to be telling them who did it. He felt insulated from it all in his high refuge and as he looked around, he decided that things might escalate further. Over by the garages he saw two mopeds on their sides. Although he couldn't see from where he was, he suspected a closer examination would reveal their tanks had been emptied into glass milk bottles. A petrol-soaked rag inserted in the top would complete the improvised weapon and he was sure two mopeds worth of petrol would make more than one petrol bomb. There was more to happen that night. He chuckled again at the irony of it all. Grub had booked him to drive them up to Harvey Nichols for "a few cocktails". Around a mile away from where he would pick them up, he could get all the cocktails he wanted...Molotov Cocktails!

Delroy had enjoyed the brief interlude but now had more important things to concentrate on. He drew his black-out curtains, returned to his bed, swallowed the last piece of pattie and put his headphones back on. Cranking up the volume another notch he was once again deep into Nelson and Frank's artistry.

CHAPTER 27

In the days following John's big trade there was some display of contrition on his part, but if you blinked you would probably have missed it. He was soon back to his old ways and was immensely looking forward to finally getting to see "Ol' Blue Eyes" live. There weren't many people in the office he hadn't told and on this particular morning Chopper gave him a knowing wink, tapped the side of his nose and conspiratorially said "Do-be-do-be-do tonight son, eh?" On a regular day you might think this was a totally normal post-lunch comment from the hapless trader who was almost at the end of his notice period, but John did get the "Strangers in the Night" reference and smiled back in agreement. Part of his anticipation was around parading Penelope in front of Grub and also impressing her with the level of entertainment he was providing (albeit not paying for).

Since he bought the SNCF bonds he had been trying, to no avail, to place them with a customer, but his only success had been with Nicola, who got rid of $10m for him as promised.

"It's the call feature on them John. Lots of my guys won't buy callable bonds because of the negative convexity".

John wasn't totally clear what negative convexity was but was hardly likely to admit it to a salesperson.

Some bonds are issued with the borrower, in this case SNCF, having the right to buy back the bonds after a set date at a pre-designated price. The object of this was to give the borrower the chance, should a large move in interest rates occur, to buy back and re-issue their debt at a better level. John had bought the bonds at a price of $96.25; the call price on them was at $102.5. In the years that John had been trading six whole points on a ten-year bond was a yawning gulf of price movement and as such he considered the call to be insignificant.

"Well, we've got to find some customers who do".

The day was following a familiar pattern with the exception of John foregoing any drinking at lunchtime for fear of spoiling his big night out. At 5.01 p.m. he rose from his leather chair, changed his tie for the Hermes one he'd left folded in his drawer, applied a generous amount of Givenchy after shave from the same place and was ready to roll.

Delroy was waiting in a cab space as promised and John was mightily impressed by sound of "The Lady is a Tramp" filtering through the glass partition between the driver and passengers.

"Nice one mate. You got any more of his?"

"That's all you're going to hear on the way!" promised the laid-back cabbie. "Extra special service, eh?"

John settled back and didn't have to wait long for the passenger side of the cab to descend by about three inches as its suspension coped with the additional weight of Grub.

"Let's go then!"

The journey to Knightsbridge was reasonably free of traffic and by 17.30 p.m. they were ascending the lift to the renowned West End watering hole known for its exclusivity and high Sloane ranger content.

As they emerged from the lift and approached the bar John looked around at the décor.

"Bit old fashioned, isn't it?" was John's first take. "Not sure about all them flowers over the walls either"

A voice from behind him made him jump somewhat. In an unmistakeable French accent, the waiter began a speech that John was sure had been trotted out many times before due to the smoothness of the delivery. "Those are Japanese Anemones Sir, inspired by the designs on Perrier Jouet Belle Epoque Cuvee. It's after the Art Nouveau style. If you'd like I can bring you a bottle"

"Yeh, why not? Ship it in shag" replied John, with the merest of looks at Grub to see if such extravagance was OK on his credit card. "I'm sure Penny will have some".

The waiter ushered them over to a small table against the side wall and proceeded to go through an elaborate ceremony of preparing an ice bucket and displaying the ornate etching on the bottle to both of them before finally uncorking the elegant bottle and pouring it first into Grub's glass. As the fine mousse effervesced up to the top of his glass John decided to help the waiter by tipping his glass to stop the Champagne bubbling up too much.

In an even more pronounced French accent the waiter looked appalled.

"Please don't tip ze glass sir, zis is not lager".

Chastened, John straightened the glass and thought to himself "prissy fucker, what's his problem?"

As soon as the waiter had placed the bottle on ice and retreated to the bar the pair raised and clinked their glasses before downing most of the glass in a single gulp.

"Tell you what, it's nice though "Grub commented through a mouthful of mixed nuts that the waiter had also left on the table." Might have to get another one of them".

Penelope was only 10 minutes late for the rendezvous but on her arrival the second bottle of champagne had already been requested and another glass acquired. John was not surprised at the look of incomprehension on Grub's face when he introduced Penelope; she looked so nice, how could he not be taken aback by her appearance. His concentration on Grub's expression was such that he completely missed a similar one on his girlfriend's face. Both of his drinking companions were certain they had met one another before, and both were equally certain that letting John know about the circumstances of their meeting was contrary to their objectives. The time it took them to work this out explained the look of uncertainty, but having arrived at a similar conclusion in a similar time the spell was broken, and Grub reached his hand out to shake hers and their smiles were reapplied to their faces.

"Nice to finally meet you Penelope...John's not stopped talking about you".

She gracefully accepted his compliment and sipped on the chilled champagne, her brain still running through her last meeting with Grub.

Grub had made a business trip to Tokyo a year ago. Although the majority of London and New York trading houses used Hong Kong as a location for trading during the Asian session, banks with a large Japanese customer base felt it was a necessary to show commitment by having a trading hub in Tokyo. When a couple of London traders who were good customers of Plummer's were assigned out there Kevin ordained that Grub should go out to see them.

He'd found it difficult out there to be honest. Japan in 1986 was still only just opening up to non-Japanese influences. It was not as if they were anti-European as such but more anti anything that wasn't Japanese. The "Sakoku" (closed country) policy meant contact with the outside world was almost totally prevented until well into the nineteenth century. Opinions vary on its effect on Japanese society but "Gaijin" meaning foreigner or outsider was an appellation used on anyone but a true born "Nihonjin" (Japanese person).

His social graces weren't strong, and in a society where a handshake was considered a little unsanitary, he was completely unsure of how to act when meeting Japanese colleagues of the Europeans he had travelled out to entertain. He was warned about the importance of treating a Japanese person's business card with more respect than he would back home and by the end of the trip had got used to bowing in response to the inclined head of the guys he would meet. One thing was certain, he was glad to reach the final day and by way of a celebration he decided to treat himself (and the three clients) to something a bit more raunchy.

"Where can we get a bit of action tonight, Graham?"

Grub had covered Graham in London for a couple of years and got on well with him. He was an outlier in terms of expats in Tokyo in that he had recently married a Japanese girl and spoke passable Japanese.

"Leave that to me Grub, there's a place in Roppongi you'll like! You know Sato-San and Ishikawa-San are down for the gig too?"

The prospect of some scantily clad women at the end of his arduous trip cheered him up immensely and he was in a very buoyant mood as he handed the cab driver another of the handwritten destination slips that Graham had carefully written in Japanese script for him. He wasn't sure where he'd end up if he tried pronouncing some of these names himself.

Graham was standing outside the office as he got out of the cab and Grub was introduced to Graham's two colleagues. He'd been told it was polite to ask a person something about their business card when exchanging them but for the life of him he didn't see much room for questions when he couldn't read anything but the numbers. With feigned interest he held each one for a couple of seconds in his hand before placing them carefully into a recently bought card holder. He was pretty sure he would consign it to the back of the desk as soon as he was back in White's Row.

The two Japanese co-workers wondered why he stood for ages looking at the Japanese side of the card when, if he had flipped it around, he could have read it all in plain English. Strange these Gaijin.

"Where we off to mate?" Grub enquired.

"A bit of nosebag first then on to Roppongi"

Against his expectations Grub had quite enjoyed Japanese food. A robata grill restaurant he had eaten in had provided some of the best barbecued food he had ever tasted, and the sashimi was a revelation. The closest he'd ever got to raw fish before this was the odd pickled herring from Brick Lane, but he could have hoovered up much more of the toro he sampled if there had been any left over. Obviously for a man of Grub's proportions, in a country where the average stature was somewhat less developed, the only place he was likely to be completely sated was the nearest sumo training camp.

It also occurred to him that they seemed to share a quality with the Germans of Schadenfreude. An enjoyment of other people's discomfort or pain. He had watched The

Clive James Show at home with clips of a Japanese game called "Za Gaman" translated as "Endurance", where a lot of people were subjected to all sorts of humiliations whilst the hosts collapsed in hysterics. Even the purpose of the Karaoke bar he'd been in seemed to be to drag someone up there so that the rest of his colleagues could mock their poor singing. Perhaps he was onto something. A love of Schadenfreude, a record of extreme punctuality on trains, and a reputation for flawless manufactured goods ...perhaps here laid the seeds of their alliance with Germany in the Second World War. How on earth did the Italians get involved in that Troika?

Once again Grub, or Grub-San as the two Japanese bankers insisted on addressing him, enjoyed his food, and even when they tried to shock him with some eels for one of the courses, he laughed it off and thought to himself "I'm from the East End guys. I could eat these all day!"

When they arrived at the hostess club, he was very impressed. Graham lined up a few hostesses and the two Japanese guys were soon pouring their hearts out to two diminutive Japanese girls who were dressed quite demurely for the type of establishment they were in. Two more women came and sat with Graham and grub." Hi, I'm Penelope, how are you?" was the greeting from the taller of the two.

Grub was very pleased with his allocated partner and as the night went on, he made it increasingly clear how he wanted the night to end. She was equally insistent that this was not on the menu and when he finally got his head round that, he found her very easy to talk to.

The night ended when Ishikawa-San collapsed, and Graham decided that he and Grub ought to shepherd him and Sato-San out to a taxi. Both lived in a suburb of Tokyo called Takanawa. When he had asked earlier in the evening how long it took to get home on the train they replied as one "take an hour". Grub wasn't sure whether to laugh or not, and suspected it was a set-up, but they kept dead pan faces.

If Graham had wanted to bat on Grub would have, but with a flight early next morning he bid farewell and got his own cab to the Imperial Palace Hotel where he was staying.

CHAPTER 28

The cab ride from Harvey Nicks to the Albert Hall was extremely short, and on entry to the box Grub introduced John and Penelope to the other customers and brokers using it. John was lapping it up, a superior position above all the general public and canapes being handed round further enhanced the experience. The wine was flowing too and before long Liza Minelli was out doing her thing. Penelope thought she was riveting, obviously born to be a performer, and although she didn't know much about Judy Garland, Liza was obviously a chip off the old block. Straight on her tail came Sammy Davis Jr. He was another natural entertainer and even managed to fit in a Michael Jackson cameo with a moonwalk included. Towards the end of his act John decided that if he wanted to see every second of Frank Sinatra's performance, he'd best visit the toilets now.

"Two seconds, just going to spend a Penny!". A wan smile passed her lips at his attempted humour, and she turned back to the stage. Her concentration was far from the stage though, the moment the self-closing door snapped back on the latch she shifted seats to sit next to Grub who had already turned to face her. "So, we meet again" Grub opened. "How long you been back from Tokyo?"

"I assume you won't be telling John about our meeting?" was her first question.

"Course not, but if you're thinking of taking things further, I wouldn't want to keep him in the dark forever" Grub's words weren't spoken as a threat but the ominous knowledge that at some point he might discover the true nature of her "dancing" was not a welcome prospect.

People talk about lightbulb moments and to Grub it looked like she'd just had one.

"You're a broker, aren't you?"

"Er yes"

"Are there many women brokers?"

Grub considered for a short time. "There's a few, here and there, but I don't think it's a game for birds. They get too emotional, can't take all the hooting and hollering. Why?"

"What's your boss like? Do you think I could see him about a job?"

At this point a rattle on the door handle signalled John's return to the box. Thankfully for Penelope the handle was a bit sticky, so by the time he had opened it she was safely back in her original seat.

John had returned just in time and as the band struck up a familiar opening, she appeared engrossed in the ageing superstar in front of her. Music was far from her mind. She was mentally grappling with why she had suddenly blurted that out to Grub.

It wasn't completely unconsidered really, in her old job many of the men she listened to were more than happy to talk to her about their work. She concluded that there might be a degree of technical knowledge necessary for a trader but couldn't understand what special powers or knowledge a broker had apart from how to handle people, and that was something she felt supremely confident in.

Similarly, Grub was intently staring at the band but thinking about what she'd just said. He would consider his boss Kevin as old school, but was he being fair to him? He had the foresight to employ someone who everyone thought was gay, he believed you had to have a diversified broker team if you wanted to cover all of a diversified client base. Perhaps a woman on the team was another step in that direction and would pick up some of the business they were currently missing? He was sure that if she played it right there'd be a fair few clients who thought a few big trades would be the way into an" enhanced" relationship. If she could keep them all at arms' length it could be a very profitable hire. The only fly in the ointment was Fieldy.Grub wasn't about to give him up as an account, and how would Fieldy react to Penelope turning up as a broker at Plummer's if he discovered Grub had been the catalyst for it?

Totally unaware of the mental turmoil going on either side of him John was well into the concert. The finale was

"New York, New York" and as the final encore was played, he looked round at Penelope as if to say, "How about that then?"

Penelope's smile was wide and genuine. The event had been most enjoyable. She had planned to stay at his after the concert, but since the incident in the box she decided she wanted to be alone with her thoughts. John looked a little crestfallen but accepted it and Grub was busy at the back of the box getting all their coats ready. If she didn't know better, she would have thought he was searching through her coat pockets as he made a big show of turning it up the right way before handing it to her. They accompanied her outside and Grub hailed a cab, gave the driver £25 and told him to take her where she wanted. As the taxi drove westward and the men waited for the next orange "For Hire" sign, she felt somewhat guilty putting her hand in her pockets to check. As far as she knew there was nothing in them originally anyway. The freshly manicured nails of her left hand snagged on something thin in her pocket. After retrieving it, and turning it around the right way, she realised it was Kevin Connolly's business card.

.

CHAPTER 29

John Field was not one for sensing mood changes. His empathy meter was somewhere down around the zero mark and if anyone really thought he would ever interpret any behavioural signals, they were optimistic to say the least. Even such an insensitive person though would have realised that since the concert Penelope's attention and involvement in their relationship had started to cool. It was worse for him somehow because of the time of year. Having reached July, markets traditionally stayed quiet until Labor Day (September). Traders with families are confined to taking time off during school breaks and desks tend to be half staffed or manned by juniors with their wings clipped as regarding trading sizes and risk limits. He could have escaped the office earlier during this period and with the long nights, the possibilities would have been endless. However, most times he suggested something Penelope would make barely believable excuses and he'd end up gambling on Sporting Index or getting drunk with his brokers.

The old saw, "Idle hands do the devil's work", could have been written for him. With less shouts coming from the broker lines due to the decreased market volume he was more likely to leave his desk and maraud around the bond floor generally annoying people, particularly after a liquid lunch. It was on one such raid he found himself standing in front of two empty chairs just around the desk from his. Alistair, one of the other traders, was abroad with his young family and his desk was uncharacteristically tidy. John caught sight of a neatly folded copy of "The Sun" which must have been from Alistair's last day at work. The conscientious cleaners, being unwilling to dispose of something the over-emotional traders might say was "essential paperwork" had dutifully folded it and left it by his telephone keyboard. The front page headlined described the latest atrocity by the IRA, an ever-present concern at that time. John glanced up over to the other side of the desk where two salespeople were idly chatting to one another. A mischievous smile began to curl at the corners of his mouth, and he pressed one of the buttons on Alistair's console to get an outside line. He carefully dialled the number for Regal Bank's bond sales team and thought to himself "let's see which one of the lazy bastards picks up first". It was hardly a surprise to him that Nicola was the first body to move towards a handset over the other side of the room and as she answered John moved as far away from the desk as possible and turned his back so they could not see or hear him speak.

"Hello, Regal Bank, Nicola Avery speaking, how can I help?"

He hesitated a moment, he had hoped it would be someone else, but after a short pause he replied, affecting his best Irish accent, "Dere's a bomb in the building, you've got tirty minutes".

He immediately hung up and surreptitiously turned to see the clamour he was expecting to have caused. "Give 'em five minutes running round like headless chickens and I'll let them off the hook" he inwardly chuckled.

There were few signs of panic from Nicola though. He saw her place the phone down momentarily and without moving her head, look right and left at her colleagues before picking the handset up again and dialling.

"Danny, I've just received a bomb threat from someone with an Irish accent. What do you advise?"

Danny Lyons was the bank's security officer. He was ex-army and had done two tours in Northern Ireland. More importantly, on his second tour, Nicola's older brother, a Sandhurst graduate, was his commanding officer.

Maybe because of this, or just Danny's Army conditioning, she had given up telling him to call her Nicola and his reply was unruffled and businesslike.

"It maybe a hoax Ma'am, but our first priority is to evacuate the building and call the Police and the bomb squad. The alarm will sound soon, please try to make everyone act calmly an obviously let nobody know about this. Do you know what time the call was Ma'am? The Police will want the recording".

"Yes Danny. 15.08 on an outside line."

"Thanks Ma'am. That means we have 27 minutes."

Across the desk John was still looking for signs of panic but apart from a slightly austere look on Nicola's face he could detect none. This wasn't turning out like he had hoped, and he came to the conclusion he should go over there and confess. There was little time for that. An ear-piercing fire alarm started going off all over the building which was greeted by most of the floor as just another drill but nevertheless a mandatory exercise. Sid the postman emerged in a high vis jacket and started shepherding people towards the fire doors. John was getting deeper in now, but how could he stop the exodus? In an orderly fashion the throng of people bottle necked at the double doors and then tramped down to the ground floor where there were more company fire wardens in more high vis tabards directing people to the assembly area. They all had to walk past Danny at the front door, surveying the exiting employees as if he were still on the parade ground. There was no way he could know anything, but Fieldy still avoided his eye. The evacuation had been quite smooth up until the point an army unit with "bomb disposal" and several fire engines joined the three squad cars already herring boned outside the building. The melee was made worse by neighbouring buildings disgorging people onto the street too. An explosion in any confined metropolitan space such as Copthall Avenue would mean related damage nearby, glass cascading down from the many windows around and the explosion funnelled upwards by the steep sided buildings. It looked like the end of a football game on London Wall.

Their usual assembly point was Finsbury Circus, a rare grass oasis in the middle of the Square Mile where avid sun lovers would gather on sunny days at lunchtime exposing every inch of skin they decently could to try to offset the effects of sitting behind a video screen for 9 hours a day. They were usually lined up on one side of the park facing the sun. Directly opposite would be a line of seedy guys with their backs to the sun and wearing dark glasses, "Nonces' Hill" the small grassy knoll was nicknamed. Did the guys think the girls didn't know what they were doing there? John was in the habit of popping into the old, wooden boarded wine bar "The Pavilion" on previous fire drills, so he headed straight there and called Grub.

"What you doing mate? Fancy a quickie in the Pavilion? Need to have a chat."

John desperately needed to unload on someone.

"Well, it aint ideal, but I suppose I could make it up there. Fuck all going on".

"Lovely. Want a Becks?"

"Yes mate, line 'em up!" For a microsecond Grub imagined Fieldy might actually be buying him a drink, but after some consideration he concluded when he got to the bar there would be a tab started that he would be expected to pick up at the end. Some traders were in the habit of calling their brokers their "wallets". They weren't far wrong really.

It took him a while to reach the Pavilion and there was an empty bottle already next to Fieldy. " Sorry mate ,took me ages. Old bill everywhere. Think there's a bomb scare."

Over the next 10 minutes Grub's lower jaw seemed to lapse lower and lower as he took in the details of John's misfiring prank.

"They're going to listen to the tapes. Where did you call them from?"

John was busy going through it all in his head. "I called on an outside line, they won't listen to any outgoing lines surely? It's only the call in the police will listen to. I used an Irish accent for that".

Grub thought to himself he'd pay good money for that recording but kept his opinions to himself.

"Let's hope nobody heard you" Grub took a large swig of cold lager and despite trying to stop himself couldn't help saying, with an ill-disguised smile on his face, "could I hear your Irish accent though John?"

John's face spoke a thousand words as did his middle finger, which he brandished in Grub's face.

The confusion caused by the emergency services meant Penelope was 10 minutes late on her arrival at Plummer's and hoped it wouldn't influence her interview with Kevin. She had stared at his card a few times before plucking up the courage to call him and arrange an interview. She called it an interview, but it was termed as a "chat" by Kevin and seemed a very informal way to embark on a career in finance for her. He had not asked for any educational provenance, or career history (although Grub had probably briefed him on that already) and though she desperately wanted to prepare for the meeting she really didn't know how to.

She felt she was getting the once over from the moment she presented herself at reception. A young girl behind a large desk seemed to look her up and down critically before asking how she could help.

"I'm here to see Kevin Connolly".

The mention of the boss's name seemed to induce a little more professionalism in the receptionist, and she promptly rose from the desk and took Penelope through the glass screen behind her and showed her to a seat outside Kevin's office. The walk from reception to the office was like a duck shoot. To her left the assembled cohorts of Plummer's brokers turned as one to watch the two ladies without the slightest tinge of embarrassment. She had dressed reasonably conservatively, in line with what her idea of a finance professional should wear, the girl in front of her looked like she was going to a party. High heels, a short skirt. Penelope wasn't sure which one of them was being leered over, but it felt uncomfortable and feral. She was glad of the cover of a large bamboo pot plant when she finally sat down. It wasn't long before Kevin put down the phone and opened the door to invite her in.

"Come in Penelope"

Kevin held the door as she entered the office and closed it carefully behind her. She felt mightily relieved to be out of sight of the wolf pack and gracefully sat down and crossed one leg over the other as Kevin took his place opposite her.

Looking back, she understood why Kevin called it a "chat". At the end of it she felt she hadn't had a chance to bring up half the things she had wanted to mention and wondered how he could offer her a job based on what had just taken place. What she didn't really appreciate was how much the business was a face-to -face thing. Business trips where people just spent some time with one another were common and in a milieu where trusting your counterpart was vitally important, just getting "a feel "for someone was an abstract, but necessary requirement.

Kevin signalled an end to the meeting by rising and showing her towards the door. "Fool" she told herself. "Why did you think you could swan up here and walk into a job without any qualifications. Get real!"

As she turned to shake hands with Kevin at the door, he was first to speak. "Nice to meet you Penelope. When you free?"

She wasn't sure what he was getting at. Was this another interview? A date?

"What do you mean?"

She looked unsure of herself.

"Could you start Monday?" His request was met with an incredulous face.

"Erm...yes!"

"Done "growled Kevin. "Get here at seven.... you'll have to work with someone to start off with, probably Veg...he's harmless. Don't suppose you've got a P60 from that Tokyo knocking shop, have you?"

"I'll bring my National Insurance number in. There's something else Kevin too".

"Shoot" he said.

"Penelope was my professional name. I'm Rita, Rita Jarvis".

"Well, I don't give a monkey's what you call yourself, you'll probably get a nick name in short order anyway. As long as you're raking in the bro, we're good".

"Oh, and another thing, bring some bacon rolls in with you Monday ...always goes down well with the troops".

The self-consciousness she felt on the walk to his office seemed to have disappeared and although she was aware of some eyes still turned to her, things were different now. These were her colleagues, she even allowed herself a little self-satisfaction as she passed the receptionist on the way out. "She's just window dressing. I've got a proper job here".

As she walked up towards Liverpool Street station, the reality of what was happening sunk in. A new wardrobe was a priority (although judging by the receptionist perhaps a few of her old work outfits would be appropriate) and more importantly she had to find a way to tell John. That wasn't going to be an easy conversation. Another necessity was lodgings nearer to town; 7 a.m. starts weren't too difficult but commuting from somewhere like her Mum's house would put a lot of hours on her days, and any late nights would be easier to handle if she was close by. The money she had stockpiled from Tokyo would be for a flat somewhere. East of town was favourite, with its cheap property prices and easy access. That was settled. Rental agent first then a trip to a department store for some respectable clothing.

CHAPTER 30

The conversation with John went more easily than expected. He seemed more upset by what he saw as Grub's "betrayal" in organising a job for her rather than worrying about her being a broker. Somehow the attraction was fading. Her hair was a slightly less strident blonde now and her new clothing range didn't seem to sit so well with the original impression he had of her.

"I think you're mad though Pen. We could have got married, kids, nice house in the suburbs. A twenty-minute ceremony and you could have had half of a £500,000 house".

"Isn't that half of a £450,000 mortgage?" she cheekily asked.

"Granted, but I'm having a good year, soon get that down."

"Good, I'm pleased for you John. One other thing, it's not Penelope anymore, it's Rita".

John regarded her as if was seeing her for the first time. "Rita? That's a shit name. Why did you change it?"

"It's my real name. I just used Penelope for work".

"Well don't expect no biz from me Rita. I've got a broker."

"No problem, John. I didn't expect it".

They sat for a while eyeing their empty wineglasses before John turned around to face her and said, "I wish you good luck Pen, er Rita. One thing's for sure, you don't have to be a rocket scientist for the old broking game, but you aint gonna look that slim for long if you're any good at it". He gestured at the empty glasses, "You picking the tab up? You're a broker now!"

"I've just started, and they haven't given me a card yet, but I don't mind." She summoned the bartender and settled the bill with cash.

The change from cossetted girl friend to entertainment sponsor was going to take a bit of getting used to but in a way that was part of what attracted her to the job. She had earned her own money in Tokyo, and she would do that here too. In a different way admittedly but somehow the reversion to her birth name was part of her metamorphosis. Penelope wasn't that girl, but Rita was.

When they left the wine bar they walked in different directions and in a way, to Rita it signified the final parting of the ways. She was glad to get back to the hustle and bustle of Plummer's and although there wasn't much going on post lunch that day, she settled down next to Veg for the next stage in her "induction".

It didn't take long for her to realise that the job was easier than she thought in some ways and a lot harder in others. In a week she reckoned she had learned as much technical knowledge as was necessary and probably exceeded half the people on the floor because she kept asking questions if she didn't understand something. Not understanding something was the last thing most people in the City would admit to. She wasn't supposed to know anything so felt no awkwardness in asking.

What she couldn't believe was the outrageous behaviour of some of the traders. How could men say women were over-emotional when she witnessed some of the "toys out of the pram" incidents that occurred in her first couple of weeks. Her estimation of the opposite sex, jaundiced as it was by her experiences in Tokyo, plumbed further lows, but her people skills meant she quickly realised how to handle conflict, how to massage their egos, how to get a trade.

By the end of a month of understudy, Kevin indicated it was time for her to cover accounts on her own. Unsurprisingly she got given all the ones that nobody wanted because they were doing little to no volume with them. Uncomplainingly she accepted the burden and resolved to get out to see them all in turn. Her appearance, and her rarity as a woman broker, meant face to face contact was a vital necessity for her to embark upon. She was also delegated as second cover on a few lines for when the main broker was out of the office. One of those was Fieldy's. She sincerely hoped Grub didn't have any vacation planned.

CHAPTER 31

L abor Day in the U.S. (the first Monday in September) normally marked resumption of normal market conditions. Things were busy but uneventful. Grub was getting fatter, John was making some good money, and Rita was getting noticed as she started accumulating accounts and writing bigger and bigger tickets. The market was friendly, especially to equity players, to whom it seemed the Dow Jones was a one-way bet. As September dwindled in the rear-view mirror John looked forward to the next U.S. holiday in his year, Columbus Day.

US holidays meant he could normally disappear for the whole afternoon and not have to rush his lunch. Two hours was definitely not long enough for a proper lunch. The absence of a need to return to the office meant he could try places further afield. This Columbus Day was celebrated in Rules, Covent Garden. The oldest restaurant in London. It was a bastion of traditional British fare like Jugged Hare and Jam Roly-Poly and as such, highly revered by John. When they exited on to Maiden Lane John had to pull his coat tight around him against the increasingly wintery weather. September had been unexpectedly mild, so the contrast was noticeable. The weather deteriorated through the week and by Thursday it was becoming very windy. That night John actually looked out of his window as he pulled his curtains to see various bits of rubbish strewn across the street, a "For Sale" sign from a nearby house pointing across the street, parallel with the ground and a few plastic dustbin lids flying around like frisbees. John tutted and hoped the winds wouldn't keep him awake.

He needn't have worried. He slept well, in fact he was quickly aware that he had slept far too well. The mole like existence of City workers at this time of the year meant none of them were used to waking in the daylight. He couldn't see the sun, but he knew it was later than usual. He turned his head around to look at his bedside alarm clock. The red LED display was flashing 00:00 at him suggesting there had been a power cut. He became aware of the winds that were gusting outside and went to the window. The sight that greeted him was pure devastation. The limp "For Sale "sign was nowhere to be seen. His neighbour's BMW wouldn't be going anywhere as there was a large oak planted square across the roof, the windscreen smashed as the structure failed to stand up to the impact.

He was later to find out about similar devastation all over the South of England, but for now he was supposed to be at work. He picked his landline up to see if it was working. Luckily, he got a dialling tone.

"Regal Bank". It was the unmistakable tones of Gary Davis.

"Gazza, it's Fieldy. What's going on?"

"It's carnage mate. I walked in but there's hardly anyone here.

"Is Rupert in yet?" John asked.

"Nah, want me to get him to call you?"

"Yes please mate...on my home number".

John was obviously not aware at the time, but the storm of October 15th/16th was a once in a generation event. Everywhere people were waking up to similar scenarios and when Rupert finally got in touch, he assured him that as it was a Friday and London was, for all intents and purposes, closed. He could stay at home.

"We'll see you on Monday John. Don't bother to come in today".

Now dressed and showered John was at a loose end. He put a pair of wellingtons on and grabbed a waxed Barbour coat and decided to go and have a look at the aftermath of the storm. He reached the little cluster of shops at the end of his road in five minutes, and it seemed he had been lucky that his electricity was on. The newsagent had a few hurricane lamps hanging to provide light. He bought a copy of the Sun, and the Indian shopkeeper asked him if he wanted an ice cream.

John was about to give the downcast looking shopkeeper a mouthful for asking a stupid question, but an explanation quickly followed.

"My freezer's been off for hours. You can have as many as you like."

Fieldy felt a pang of guilt and hoped the guy was covered by insurance.

"Sorry to hear that mate. I'll have a couple of Magnums please".

John spent the rest of the day looking at TV news. The enormity of what had happened became clearer as the day went on and he guessed the guy with the BMW had to think himself lucky he wasn't in the car when the oak fell.

CHAPTER 32

Monday 19th October dawned without any special portents of the cataclysm to come. The morning was relatively quiet, but when New York opened John, along with all the other participants in the market, were witnesses to a remarkable event. Black Monday as it was soon dubbed saw the DJIA down 22.6 % and fixed income markets spiking up massively (down in yield) as traders handled the flight to quality flows and the expectations of Central Bank rate cutting to come. You can read a multitude of reasons for the event, relatively new black-box trading couldn't handle the volume, insurance claims to come from the storm meant liquidation of assets by insurance companies provided more selling etc, etc. The truth is that equity markets had been under pressure all the preceding week and when it comes down to it, as experienced traders would trot out when devoid of reasons; "there were more sellers than buyers".

That statement is not inaccurate, but fails to illustrate the factor by which there were too many sellers. It's true that the algorithms for the recently introduced black boxes functioned without emotion. Buy something, it goes down by a certain amount, sell it again. Humans at some point will say" hold on, this must stop somewhere." The early trading systems weren't programmed like that.

People talk about Black Monday, but Tuesday wasn't a whole lot better, and it was Wednesday before traders felt they could sit down and work out where all their prices were following the massive upheaval in their underlying markets, U.S. treasuries.

All the bonds John traded, as with his rivals, used US treasury bonds as their benchmarks. Simply explained, if you owned a 10-year bond for say EIB (European Investment Bank), and the price was 96.5/97 and the US 10-year bonds went up half a point, the EIB were moved up by the same amount to 97/97.5.

This is a massive oversimplification, but hopeful demonstrates the relationship between the bonds John traded and the underlying US treasury bonds.

Big moves in US treasuries were things like one whole point in a day. As John tried to mark his bond prices to somewhere near a realistic level on Wednesday, he was facing moves of eight points or so.

The systems around at the time made this a somewhat time-consuming endeavour and little trading took place on the Wednesday because everyone was in the same boat apart from those with more advanced systems. Nobody wanted to trade with the advanced system guys because it was feared they might have more idea where things were than the rest of the market.

Tentative price levels were arrived at in some sporadic trading on Thursday and Friday so by Monday the following week John felt a little more comfortable about where things were.

It was halfway through Monday morning when he became aware of someone standing behind him with a file of papers in his hands. John hadn't seen him before and slowly spun around in his chair without stopping his phone conversation to regard the visitor. Robert Vernon looked like he'd been locked in a dungeon for most of his life. An emaciated body, a pallid complexion with a few freckles dotted across his cheeks, an untidy profusion of wavy brown hair and a pair of circular spectacles made it hard for John to hide his distaste. Finishing his conversation, John placed the phone down an addressed the newcomer.

"I didn't know Regal Bank was haunted! You look like the local ghost!"

Robert's expression barely changed as he reached out a hand to introduce himself. "I'm Robert from product control. I only started a couple of weeks ago. Do you think I could have a word about one of your prices?"

"Fancy yourself as a market-maker, do you? "John's tone was immediately more aggressive at the prospect of some back-office twat trying to tell him where things should be. Did he expect a market to be functioning properly after what happened last week?

"Listen, if something's half a point out here or there after last week's shit show I don't think it's the end of the world. Which issue you want to talk about?"

Robert leafed through the wad of paper he had and extricated a single sheet.

"These SNCF 10year bonds. You marked them at 97 last week, this week you've marked them at 105". He emphasised the point by sliding the sheet of paper onto John's desk.

"Has it escaped your attention Hercule Poirot, that the U.S. 10 year is up over eight points since last week? John delivered this at a volume for all the floor to hear. Enjoying the public humiliation of the new guy.

Once again, Robert's demeanour hardly changed. Despite his ineffectual appearance he was completely confident in his data. He felt like shouting his reply at the top of his voice but resisted the temptation.

"Yes, but they are callable at 102.5. I think you have them marked roughly 2.5 points too high. On $120 million that means your P and L is overstated by about $3,000,000".

A feeling like ice went down John's spine. Few had seen him speechless for long, but from wanting the whole world to see his encounter with the geek from downstairs he now wanted the earth to swallow him. When John was adjusting all his prices in reaction to the huge moves of the previous weeks, he had taken all the moves on the different maturity US bonds and moved his Eurobond prices up in lockstep. 2-years up 1.5 points, 3-years up 2.5 points etc, etc. All his 10-year bonds had been moved up by the same amount as the US Treasury 10 year moved up. The call on the SNCF bonds had been so far away in price terms that he had completely disregarded it.

Ostensibly he was looking at the sheet of paper Robert had slid on the desk but really, he was going through the ramifications. His P and L was up around $3.5 million for the year. He would lose nearly all of that in one fell swoop and then have about two and a half months to make some back. Before anything else, he needed to think.

"Have you told anyone about this yet?" He questioned Robert so quietly it was hardly audible.

"No" was the reply "it just came up from some revaluation work I was doing."

"Do me a favour. Just sit on this while I have a look at it at the end of day. I'm a bit busy right now."

Fieldy's conspiratorial tone was in such contrast to his original attitude that Robert felt like chiding him about it. The temptation to put on a Belgian accent and say "perhaps I have a few more leetle grey cells than you Monsieur "was almost overwhelming, but as his ultimate aim was to get onto a trading desk himself, he thought antagonising existing traders was not the way forward.

As Robert shambled away, Fieldy got straight on the phone again. Well, he picked it up and put it to his ear, but there was nobody at the other end. He could feel the eyes of his colleagues on him and didn't want to be questioned about what had just happened. His head was still whizzing around like a cornered wasp. If he could keep Mr Vernon quiet for a little while he could perhaps start edging the valuation in a bit and nobody would notice. If the US 10year came down 2.5 points he'd be fine...they would be right again. He would have to tell Rupert at some point. He glanced across to the office. It was empty and he remembered Rupert was at some AIBD conference, returning tomorrow. AIBD was the acronym for the Association of International Bond Dealers. The last two letters soon came to stand for Beer Drinkers after some of the meetings. Fieldy decided he wouldn't do anything yet. It was justifiable in his opinion to wait for Rupert's return to the office to give such a bad piece of news. Who knows? If the market crapped out big time overnight, he wouldn't need to say anything. The rest of his day was spent avoiding contact with others in the room and at 5.01 p.m. he slipped out of his chair (purposely this time rather than as a result of the shiny leather) and recovered his coat as inconspicuously as possible before leaving the building without saying goodbye to anyone. The cold October air and the walk to the Underground station made him look around at all the people sharing the pavement with him. He wondered if any of them had anything on their minds like the turmoil going on in his head. How could they? They were mere office clerks most likely, safe in their day-to-day routine, the crushing banality of which was suddenly appealing to John. As he reached the stairs to descend to the Underground, he looked down the stairs and saw the figure of his nemesis, Robert Vernon about ten yards ahead of him.

It seems he was heading for the same line as John. The rush hour commuters were crammed together on the narrow platform and for a few moments the thought of how easy it would be to shove the unsuspecting analyst on to the track in front of an oncoming train. The reasons for not doing it were by no means headed by "you can't kill someone just to hide a P and L fuck up". If that would solve the problem John was prepared to countenance it, but Robert might have told someone else, and it would all have been in vain. John would perhaps not have been aware, but this pattern of thought would probably have given him a free entry into "Psychopaths Anonymous" but sadly that's how he was wired. There was nothing else to do. He would have to make the walk of shame into Rupert's office tomorrow on his return.

"Fuck... fuck fuck fuck!"

CHAPTER 33

Just as bonus rounds were a recurring punctuation mark in the cycle of capital markets, so were mass redundancies. Periodically companies came to a realisation that after non-stop binges of hiring, and awarding themselves large packages, the sums just weren't adding up. "Eureka, let's sack a load of people who aren't us!" To say companies had no qualms about this process would be untrue but it would also be accurate to say that one of their biggest concerns was to not be seen as hard-hearted about the manner of the announcements. Losing your job just before Christmas was considered beyond the pale in the unwritten etiquette of mass redundancies so November was the last month of the year when it would be considered.

Rupert surveyed the list in front of him with Chuck Henderson's "recommended rationalisation list". He didn't agree with the widespread cuts outlined but all pushback from him had been vigorously rejected by his American boss and now it was coming up to the time for action. It didn't help that Chuck's attitude to "taking these guys out" sounded more like a CIA black ops operation. Rupert hated this aspect of his job. You would really have to despise someone to enjoy giving them their marching orders, and he had no such animosity for anyone on his team.

The main problem companies had was the fact that none of these announcements were ever a secret. The prospect of upcoming redundancies always seemed to get into the public domain before announcement and the speculation would start much like the pre-bonus betting. Different companies had tried different methods over the years of informing a disparate group of people, who arrived at the office at varying times and sometimes were on vacation, of their obsolescence simultaneously with sufficient compassion for the situation. Mostly they got it massively wrong, but their hearts were in the right place. One Firm adopted an "X" Factor scenario. As people arrived at work, they were told to go to either one floor or another. When everybody had finally arrived at work one group were more or less told they were "through to the next round" whilst the other group received the news that they "didn't make it to Judges' houses".

In one case the Bank decided, in a moment of divine inspiration to send motorcycle couriers out on the night before D-Day with redundancy packages to employees' home addresses. This worked reasonably well in most cases, but one of the redundant staff had been out on the sauce all night. His wife refused to answer the door to a helmeted man, who had trouble finding the address, deep in the countryside and didn't arrive until 9 p.m. The banker in question finally arrived home at 11.pm and dutifully turned up for work next morning to the embarrassment of his bosses who had to send the youngest female member of HR down to tell him he didn't work here anymore. Nobody else wanted to face the hungover trader themselves and thought it was less likely to kick off with the innocent junior doing the dirty.

Generally, the exit strategy was very unceremonious. Staff who were made redundant were treated as if they had suddenly caught Yellow Fever. Re-entry into the office was forbidden and normally a cardboard box with personal effects in would have been stacked by a secretary and be available for the jettisoned staff to pick up on their way out.

Rupert of course had heard about all these incidents but in all fairness still struggled to come up with a satisfactory method of proceeding. He was going to have to get on with it soon.

In the trading room, John sat regarding Rupert. The redundancies were also the topic of concern on his mind. His revelations about the SNCF loss last month had been treated as well as he could have hoped for by Rupert but had John just put himself in the crosshairs?

As if he felt John's gaze upon him, Rupert stood up and walked out of the dealing room down to the floor below to an office he had arranged to be set up for the exit interviews. The HR representative was already there with a large pile of envelopes and a suitably funereal expression painted on her face. "

"Hi Josie, suppose we've got to get on with this".

He sat down at the desk next to her and picked up the first envelope and began.

He found the process emotionally draining and peoples' reactions hard to predict. Some were incredulous that they couldn't even go back up to collect their coats, some men bursting into tears, but that was the way he had been instructed to conduct himself and he breathed a sigh of relief when it was finally concluded. Upstairs someone else was equally relieved. Fieldy was sure his SNCF faux pas had painted a red cross on his back but thankfully he had survived. His ability to quickly condemn any adversity to the dustbin of his memory was part of his strength as a trader so he was soon planning a way of celebrating his stay of execution. Lunchtime was beckoning.

"Grub! How do you fancy some Beaujolais Nouveau?" he shouted down the box.

In 1985 the Institut National des Appellations d'Origene established the third Thursday in November as Beaujolais Nouveau Day and City wine bars and restaurants were quick to market it as another excuse to get punters through the doors. Some stunts were organised to publicise the day, like transporting it on Concorde or via elephant but all the puff in the world couldn't disguise the fact in Grub's mind that it tasted vile.

"Yeah ok." He replied down the box. "Let's go to that French place round the corner from you".

"Do you mind if Gazza comes along? He's at a loose end".

"No problem, does he like red wine?". He'd only ever seen Gazza necking pints and found it hard to imagine him having a fondness for red wine.

"He'll drink anything if it's free" John assured him.

Grub needn't have worried. It did seem that Gazza had a capacious appetite for red wine and almost 4 bottles had been consumed by the end of the lunch. Considering Grub was on beer, the two traders, with only a Bouef Bourgignon and some mash to offset the alcohol were feeling quite woozy and given the dramatic nature of the morning John kept himself reasonably restrained, turning his leather chair around and kneeling on it with his head over the top to make it easier to cling on. For Gazza also, discretion was the better part of valour, although the ex-milkman may not have used Falstaff as his inspiration. John saw him disappear at about 3.00 p.m. and zigzag towards the toilets. Chuckling to himself he was relishing the wisdom of visiting them before he came onto the floor. When some 20 minutes had passed, he started wondering what was going on. He concluded Gazza had probably fallen asleep in there and really that was his best option. Let him sleep it off. A regular occurrence in the Gents toilet was for someone to catch a colleague in a cubicle and turn the lights off.

There were two sets of doors to enter the toilets so with the lights off the darkness was impenetrable. Perhaps he was marooned in there waiting for someone to come in and turn them on again. Suddenly a young salesman came running into trading room. He had panic written across his face and John asked,

"What's up with you Robbie? You look scared shitless?"

"It looks like the chainsaw massacre in trap two. Blood everywhere. There's no body or anything. Come quick"

John didn't really fancy trying to run in his Gamay induced stupor but made a slightly speeded up walk to follow his young colleague to the Gents.

Robbie's information that it was trap two was the most superfluous ever given. The second cubicle from the entrance was covered in a blood-red fluid. He couldn't for the life of him work out how Gazza had managed to vomit the majority of his lunch with such uniform precision on every square inch of the tiling and white Formica side walls. He looked briefly at the back of the door.

"Yep, there too!" He was surprised that one of the observations that occurred to him was the total lack of any solid matter in the discharge covering the floor. It looked like someone had just walked in there with a couple of jugs of wine and then spun around in a circle until they were empty.

He looked round at Robbie, who still looked concerned. "Don't worry about anything mate, that's not blood, it's Beaujolais!"

CHAPTER 34

With the passing of Thanksgiving Day, which was always the last Thursday in November, the edge seemed to have gone from the normal cut and thrust of trading. From this day forward, time was usually set aside for entertainment. A keen-eyed observer might justly remark that a good part of the year preceding thanksgiving had its fair share of schmoozing, but in December there were more corporate functions, end of year balls and the like.

Broking firms liked to hold big Christmas events. Some members of management were hesitant about visibly spending too much on these events for fear the market-makers might start questioning how much brokerage they were paying and lobby for lower commissions. There were a greater number of decision makers however that felt one should make hay while the sun shone and pushed for ever more lavish venues. Plummer's extravaganza this year was to be held in a vast marquee complex on the playing fields of the HAC. The Honourable Artillery Company, one of the oldest regiments in the British Army, was formed by King Henry VIII in 1537 and they were the owners of an extremely valuable green space within the City boundaries containing two football pitches, a cricket square and some more land at the end where they pitched the marquees. Plummer's hired the whole thing for this year's Christmas bash and also organised some gaming tables with croupiers for blackjack and a couple of roulette wheels. Much as they would have liked to, it was not legal for the invited guests to gamble with real money so every attendee was to be given an identical amount of chips to gamble with and there would be prizes at the end for the best three performers.

The day of the event dawned and very few of those people invited had RSVP'd with a "No". John regarded the gilt-edged ticket in his drawer with the details on. There was an individual number printed on the bottom corner of it which was labelled "Unique Raffle Number". The prize wasn't detailed on there, but market gossip suggested there was a Caribbean holiday for two waiting to be doled out to a lucky guest, amongst other branded luxuries. What would he do if he won that? All his acquaintances were from the market, the prospect of spending ten days round a pool with Grub squeezed into a pair of Speedos was not something that filled him with anticipation. Anyhow, with his luck this year he couldn't see him winning anything. To be honest he couldn't wait to get past the year end and start anew. He'd even ended up with a thousand party poppers that he didn't know what to do with. Some joker from Credit Suisse had asked him to make a market in a thousand party poppers. Obviously, any sane individual would have perhaps replied "I'm trading $ Euros, not party poppers" but such were the monumental egos of traders at the time, the concept that there could be something in the world that they couldn't put a price on was an heinous insult. John considered briefly..." I'll make you £100/£150". He'd hardly got the bid out before the guy on the other end of the line said, "yours a thousand, could do more". John said "done" and hung up. This had happened last year with Christmas trees, but he managed to sell his ten trees on for a nice turn and speedily grabbed another line to hopefully do the same with his party poppers. It soon became clear that he had made a vastly high price and concluded he would make the guy from Credit Suisse deliver them just to be stubborn. Usually, you just settled on the difference in the price. He looked down at them under his desk.... another memento of his annus horribilis. "Ah well, Plummer's tonight...I could still win a holiday!"

Rita was also looking forward to the evening. Although she had a considerable wardrobe from her Tokyo days, the outfits were all a little too revealing in her opinion. She had ventured out to Selfridges at the end of November and finally settled on an elegant black gown that she thought radiated just the vibes she was looking for. She wasn't the only one who had been out shopping. Every woman who worked in Plummer's had hung a garment carrier somewhere in the office and although there weren't many female brokers there were still plenty of women in the back office and reception staff. A look around at her colleagues confirmed that the males in the office had planned on a somewhat reduced preparation routine for the evening. They would all be going in the suit and shirt they were sitting in now. Some of them would presumably apply some after shave, perhaps a few even clean their teeth but her hopes were not high.

Over her time working next to Grub she had become quite attached to him. His ability to play the nice guy to his clients on the line and then to change as soon as he hung up, Chameleon-like, to make sarcastic remarks about their shortcomings, was always a source of amusement to her. She learnt to harbour a healthy dose of cynicism about traders' morals and motives whilst appearing very non-judgemental on the phone. He'd developed an almost paternal attitude towards her (as soon as it was clear she wouldn't sleep with him) and she felt safe when they went on client events together as he always made sure she was getting home safe.

Preparations for Rita began around 4.30 p.m. but it seemed some of her colleagues had been preening themselves all day. She arranged to meet Grub at Cozy's, a spot quite near the HAC, at around 6.30 p.m. with some other brokers. He was obviously not going to be sitting around in the office waiting for her to get ready and by 5 pm, most of the floor was empty of brokers, while the remaining women, taking advantage of the increased space to use, had spread their beauty paraphernalia wider; competing for unused power sockets to plug their hair dryers and curlers in and retrieving various potions from the make-up bags strewn across desks normally occupied by corpulent brokers.

By 6.15 p.m. Rita was satisfied with her appearance and joined two other girls who were getting a cab to the venue. They had to go right past Cozy's, so they dropped her off on the way. Before starting in the City, she might have been a bit self-conscious about wandering into a busy wine bar like this where men outnumbered women by about five to one but her sensitivity to such things had definitely diminished over the last few months and as she entered, she didn't feel at all fazed by the number of eyes turned towards her. Spotting Grub and a couple of mates she headed straight up to him and smiled as she said, "can a girl get a drink then?". Grub didn't make any move towards the bar, but one of his younger colleagues immediately ordered a glass of champagne. Grub still had his eyes fixed on her. "Fuck me, you scrub up well Rita. You look a million dollars".

"Cheers Grub" she replied, and gratefully accepted the incoming flute of Champagne. After a couple more drinks they walked the couple of hundred yards to the venue. It was mightily impressive. It took about five minutes for Rita to blow all her chips at once on a lucky number at the roulette wheel, but to be honest she hadn't come to stand by that all night and unburdened of them she headed into the main area where the dance floor was becoming quite lively already. Men dancing in suits always looked strange to her. It was very hard for them to look cool with heir jackets undone and most of them would have struggled to do them up even though double-breasted was the fashion of the day.

She'd met enough people in the market by this time to be comfortable flitting from one familiar face to another and was greeted by appreciative looks wherever she went. Despite trying studiously to evade him she somehow ended up next to John just as the music was paused and Kevin Connolly appeared next to the DJ.

Kevin made some attempt to modulate his accent but was still unmistakably East End.

"Fanks for coming everyone. Before I do the draw, I'd just like you to give your appreciation for my two secretaries who sorted this all out. I've done fuck all!"

After a warm bout of clapping and cheering he continued. "Secondly, I need to do the draw for the prizes" At this point two glamourous women emerged from side stage pushing a ridiculously old-school tombola drum containing all the ticket numbers. There were ten prizes and each time they span the drum Kevin would delve his hand in to the depths of the machine whilst the two girls stood there like magician's assistants. As the desirability of the gifts ascended, Rita was secretly hoping for the Louis Vuitton filo-fax that she had noticed listed. This was the penultimate prize, and she had a tinge of envy as she watched an old guy just about make it up the stairs to collect it from one of the girls.

"Now we have a nice surprise" Kevin continued. "As you may or may not know, there was some mumble of the last prize, the "surprise trip" being a Caribbean holiday. The mumble was right...the next ticket gets ten days for two in St Lucia!"

The DJ found a cheesy fanfare from somewhere and to the sound of trumpets Kevin extricated a number and read it out. Rita had to look twice to check, but when Fieldy looked over her shoulder and read it too it was undeniable.

"It's me!! It's me". Rita scurried across to the stage as fast her heels would allow brandishing her ticket on high and reached Kevin before he could change his mind. She never dreamed any broker would be allowed to win the main prize, but the draw must have been completely random. The DJ was already restarting the dancing with an Earth Wind and Fire classic guaranteed to get everyone going when she reached Kevin, and he handed her the voucher. "'Ere you go girl. I'm pleased for you. Who you taking?"

This was something that hadn't even crossed her mind so far. There were a few girls she got on with in the office, but by far her closest relationships were with fellow, male brokers. Her absence from the country for such a long time with her previous work meant she had no real candidates for the holiday but that was a bridge to be crossed another time. Maybe she should offer it to her Mum? That was an option that wasn't considered for long. Making sure she securely placed the voucher in her bag she gave Kevin a quick hug then shot back to the dance floor.

When the night finally came to an end she was still riding on a wave of exuberance and as the year was coming to an end it made her quite emotional to think how her prospects and attitudes had changed over the last year. With the music stopped, and dark suited security men trying to marshal everyone out of the venue, she saw Grub, propped against the bar and walked towards him.

Given the time he started drinking he was reasonably coherent still and wanted to congratulate her on her good fortune. "Well done mate. I am available if you're short of a mucker to go with!"

"You'd be ahead of a few people Grub" she smiled at him, "but I think I'll take my Mum".

"That's sweet of you. How you getting home?"

"I'll jump a taxi. No sweat" she assured him.

"Come with me, I'll get you one".

They wandered out together, picked up their coats at the makeshift cloakroom station and emerged into the crisp December air. Rita started to make her way over to the line of black cabs waiting directly outside but Grub caught her elbow and moved her in the direction of Chiswell Street. She was only slightly concerned with his insistence but at the end of the road she saw another black cab with its engine running but no orange light on and she was sure she could hear Marvin Gaye in the background.

On seeing the approaching couple, the driver lowered his window slowly.

Delroy had told Grub he'd be outside for most of the night. He'd have quite a few regular customers in the marquee tonight and he fancied demand would be high. He wasn't disappointed. Grub was lucky to catch him really. When the trail of customers tailed off, he was on the verge of going home but got stuck into some Marvin Gaye and time just flew. "What's going on" was his favourite album of all time. He wasn't normally concerned about lyrics in songs, but the sentiments expressed on this album were still as relevant now as they were in 1971. With a warm cab, and a sumptuous sound system, he hadn't been in a hurry to go anywhere.

The slowly descending window confirmed Rita's first thought. Marvin it was. "Hello Grub! What you after?"

"You finished for the night mate? Can you take this young lady home? She's in Stepney." Grub asked.

"Yes of course. Jump in love". Delroy reached his hand back through the open driver's window to open the back door.

"Here's a score. Make sure she's OK" Grub waved a £20 note at Delroy who was feeling very mellow.

"Nah, don't worry about it. I've had a good night".

Rita waved to her colleague as Delroy span the taxi round in a seemingly impossible space before heading off eastwards.

Delroy began the conversation. "Had a good night?"

Rita looked upwards with a dreamy expression "the best, and I won a holiday to the Caribbean too!"

Delroy had a sudden inspiration and at the next lights he rooted through his cassettes and slotted in one with "SOCA" written on the back. It was not an artist or song that she was familiar with but Gypsy singing Sing Ram Bam put her straight in the middle of the Caribbean. "Oh, this is great. Where's this guy from?" She asked.

"Well, he's a Trinny. A lot of the Soca music is either Trinny or Bajan, but you'll hear it all over the islands. It's only Jamaica where reggae is king".

After another few bars Delroy spoke again. "Where exactly you going on holiday?"

"Saint Lucia "she replied.

"For real? "said Delroy incredulously. "That's where my Mum's from. She's there now with my sisters."

Rita was astounded at the coincidence. "What's it like?"

"Dunno, never been."

This made her feel a little awkward and she quickly changed the subject. Their conversation flowed easily. Her chauffeur was relaxed and affable and his attitude was a world away from the testosterone charged banter she had become used to in the office. The journey to her flat was not long. In no time at all Delroy was edging his cab into the pavement outside her place in a neat Victorian square in the heart of Stepney.

"Here you go, 44A".

Rita slid her bottom forward on the seat and said through the dividing screen "are you sure I don't owe you anything for the ride?"

"Definitely not, was my pleasure. Now get indoors. Grub's told me I've got to make sure you get home OK".

She carefully opened the passenger door and stretched her toe down to the pavement carefully as she had taken her heels off on the journey. Delroy watched her slip her expensive looking fur coat over her shoulders and carefully tiptoe towards her house. He'd wound down the front window to get a good look at her. The rationale for this was not entirely to make sure she reached her front door safely. Halfway to the front door she stopped rather suddenly. A spark of memory made her think of the moment she'd blurted out her desire to be a broker on a mad impulse in the Albert Hall. In her opinion that hadn't turned out badly.

"Here goes nothing".

In a sharp movement, in contrast to the feline grace she had been exhibiting, she span round. Delroy panicked a little bit and hoped he hadn't been caught scoping her hips.

With two or three strides she was back at his cab, popping her head through the open window.

"How do you fancy ten days in Saint Lucia?"

—

Printed in Great Britain
by Amazon

41574770R00145